The Killing Spirit
A Savage Tale of Orcs

Sean-Michael Argo

PublishAmerica
Baltimore

First printing

ISBN: 1-4137-2397-7
PUBLISHED BY PUBLISHAMERICA, LLLP
www.publishamerica.com
Baltimore

Printed in the United States of America

Chapter 1

A muscle in Ma-Gur's face twitched once, the only outward sign that betrayed his discomfort. The orc tried not to flinch again as the foul smelling breath of the ugly wizard wafted through his nostrils. The orcish wizard, Ghalik, whose name was both a call sign for himself and the title of his position within the tribe, grunted derisively and continued cutting the horizontal white stripe into Ma-Gur's face.

The young orc was receiving his Blooding Mark, a unique ritual tattoo given to all orcs of the Angir tribe before they set off to become warriors. This was known to Ma-Gur and was the primary source of his discomfort. The pain in his face was almost nothing compared to the pangs of impatience and anxiety. He knew that once the tattoo was finished he would travel into the mountains with the rest of the Angir youths. There he would take part in the Blooding, a savage rite in which the youth of the tribe would battle for supremacy. In the Angir tribe supremacy meant everything from breeding rights, to food and spoils of war.

A blinding pain forcibly removed Ma-Gur from his musings. Ghalik had slapped a handful of white ashes into the tattoo as he recited ancient words of magic. Upon hearing the words Ma-Gur knew that from now on there was no going back. All of the youths had been told about the Blooding Mark. It was both a symbol and a spell, cursing its bearer to either be victorious in battle or die fighting. For an orc warrior of the Angir there was no retreat, to do so would be to invoke the power of the spell and die a horrible death, anyway, at least that was what the legends said.

The Ghalik grunted and motioned for Ma-Gur to stand and join the others as he motioned for the next young orc in line. There were about sixty all told, long-haired and muscled, straight-backed younglings who had never tasted battle beyond the playfulness of youth, which admittedly for an orc was quite rough. Once friends, many of them now eyed each other with murderous glares and barely concealed hostility.

In time Ghalik had tattooed everyone, and as he laid down his tools he motioned for the group to follow him. Without further communication the band of orcs followed the wizard out of the village and into the icy wilderness. No one spoke during the journey, as it usually was with their kind. Orcs had their own language of course, a corrupted and guttural form of the common speech used by man, elf and dwarf. Though they seldom used it, most orcish communication was accomplished through body language, posturing, and that strange bond that all orcs seemed to share.

Some believe that this was because the orcs were once the favored of the gods. Able to take part in the marvels of creation as if gods themselves. It was through pride in their own magnificence that they forgot the generosity and divinity of the gods. They abandoned the light for the sake of the darkness that comes with hubris and self-worship. They became twisted and jealous, striving to find supremacy through a war with the gods. It was in this way that the orcs came to be.

These things the wizard told the younglings as they journeyed up the old mountain pass.

"Our twisted and warped race is the remnant of these failed demigods. Driven by a lust for supremacy that consumes all other goals in life. That is why we crave battle, because only in battle does the inner might of our race become supremacy over all things," ranted the bloated Ghalik.

As he spoke his words began to fill the young orcs with a self-loathing sense of pride. These complex ideas and speeches were not lost upon their youngling minds. Orcs were by far one of the most naturally intelligent races to exist. It was their battle madness, lack of technology, and rough language that hid this fact from the rest of the world. Though at the same time Ghalik's speech was likely the longest any of the younglings had heard any orc speak at one time.

"We do not build cities because we are made to destroy, not construct. We are immortal and bear many children, but are not great in numbers. It is our curse that we live to fight, but our blessings are in our strength and our might. We of the Angir are the keepers of this knowledge, supreme over all other orcs because we know the truth. Our knowledge gives us strength, that is why all other orcs are stooped and we stand tall in the radiance of our own greatness," raved the old wizard.

The orcs began to lowly growl deep in their throats sensing the climax of the speech that would send them to their Blooding.

"We killed all those who knew. Now we are the only ones who remember. The first among orcs!" Bellowed the Ghalik as he led the group to a clearing at the peak of the mountain.

It was a circular depression in the earth that looked much like an arena. While no hands had crafted it or built upon it, the walls were smooth and flush. There was even a natural staircase leading down into the area.

"This is the proving ground of the gods," the Ghalik stated as he turned to face the group of eager and mystified younglings.

They looked about in awe as they began to notice strange things about the arena itself. For some reason the snow that covered everything as far as the eye could see did not fall upon the arena itself. Not a flake could be seen to touch the smooth stone walls and the hard packed dirt floor. As they looked at the floor of the arena the young orcs noticed a large pile of ancient and rusted weapons lying next to the bottom of the staircase. There were axes, spears, shortswords, daggers, and many other cruel and wicked tools for violence.

Noticing their hungry gaze, the Ghalik pulled a large sack from his belt as he began to address the group.

"Inside this sack are bone tokens. Each one has been dipped in a colored dye," said Ghalik as he beckoned the group to circle around him, "Each of you take one."

The young orcs all pressed forward, eagerly grasping a token and clutching it greedily. Soon the sack was empty and everyone had a small colored token.

"Now, everyone into the pit," the Ghalik instructed as he pointed towards the natural arena, "take a single weapon as you enter and then stand back against the wall."

The young orcs did as they were told, each one picking up a killing tool as they spread out inside the pit. Once all of the orcs had weapons they stood with their backs against the walls of the arena, ringing the entire area with their large numbers. As they did this the Ghalik moved along the top of the structure until he stood at what appeared to be a naturally formed stone chair. The young orcs watched as the bloated wizard hefted his bulk onto the throne.

"Each of you has a token. For every token there is a match. Find the match for your token amongst your brothers and stand with he who is your match," ordered the old wizard.

The younglings did as they were told. They held up their tokens in plain view as the sixty of them mingled about. Matches were found quickly, and soon thirty pairs of orcs stood facing Ghalik.

"As you might have guessed by now, the orc who is your match is your enemy. In order to be a warrior of the Angir you must walk on the path of your ancestors," intoned Ghalik as he drew his battle-axe and gestured towards a nearby stone pillar bearing dozens of slash marks, as if struck by a blade, "When I strike this stone you will kill your brother in mortal combat. If you survive you will be a Blooded orc warrior, and every life you take will bring you a step closer to supremacy. Until the day when the orcish kind finally dies out, and goes on to challenge the gods."

Ghalik paused for a moment as he allowed his words to take effect. He watched with morbid satisfaction as the memories of friendship and childhood camaraderie vanished in the eyes and expressions of the assembled orcs. They glowered at each other, the battle-lust mounting in their hearts.

The orc wizard let the tension build for another moment, then with a great bellow he hefted his massive waraxe and swung it with all his might towards the stone pillar. The wide blade of the axe cleft a chunk of rock away from the pillar as the sound of the blow rang out across the frozen mountaintops.

With terrifying howls of rage and battle-lust the younglings surged towards their partners. Litter-mates ran each other through with snarls of fury as one-time friends hacked and slashed each other into a great bloody mess. Within a few moments the initial frenzy of combat thinned as most of the pairs had brutally resolved their contest.

As most of the others backed away from the carnage, some still shaking with berserker fury, two combatants could be distinguished from the crowd. The remaining pair, Ma-Gur and Forglug, were still locked in deadly combat. The crowd gazed with eyes greedy from blood.

It was well known that these two orcs had been litter-mates and friends since birth. Bullies, both, given their mutual large size amongst their peers, they were generally disliked by the other younglings, but praised and encouraged by the warriors and elders of the tribe. All present were too intent upon the savage duel to notice the satisfied look upon Ghalik's face. It would be taken as a good omen that the two strongest younglings ended up paired together. No one need ever know that Ghalik had used sleight of hand to ensure the duel's arrangement. As with the orcs and their kind, prowess in battle was the basis of leadership, but Ghalik would not be who he was had he not had the gifts of cunning and foresight. By witnessing such a battle as was now taking place, the younglings would instinctually follow whoever emerged victorious. The newly emerging leader would become the captain of his Blood Brothers, those who had survived this day alongside him. So as the youth of this generation looked to him, so he would look to his leaders. Thus maintaining and furthering not only the Angir way of life, but also the instinctual orcish ideals of divine ascension as the expression of personal might.

As all orc warriors knew, and these newly Blooded warriors would know, establishing supremacy of the orc race is the most potent method of each orc to reach the true goal of individual supremacy. Watching the two younglings do battle, Ghalik and the younglings all felt as if they watched their mythical ancestors at war.

Ma-Gur contemplated none of these things. His only thoughts were strike, parry, and kill. Gone were the memories of his lifelong friendship with his litter-mate, they had been turned to ashes by the bloodlust burning in his twisted soul. The days of his camaraderie with Forglug as they picked on the other younglings were over, their bittersweet ache barely felt as Forglug turned into an object in Ma-Gur's mind. Now a nameless and hated thing, a piece of meat to be carved and discarded.

If Forglug thought any differently he did not show it as he swung his sword in a wide arc towards Ma-Gur's midsection. The other orc barely had time to parry as he brought up the shaft of his two-handed axe just in time to save himself. Unfortunately for Ma-Gur the wooden shaft was old and weak, Forglug's blade was sturdy and it's wielder strong. At the last moment Ma-Gur twisted his torso away in anticipation of the blow as the axe's shaft buckled and the heavy blade slammed into his side.

The powerful blow forced Ma-Gur to his knees as Forglug brought his sword about for another swipe. By this time both combatants were cleaved and bloody in many places. Axe and sword having tasted orcflesh several times as the battle progressed. Yet these duelists were orcs, and as such were both blessed and cursed with a tenacious single-mindedness that allowed them to carry on the fight even if near death. It was this singularity of purpose that afforded Ma-Gur with the strength to rise, despite his grievous wounds.

With a snarl of hatred, Ma-Gur rose from his knees as he attempted one last desperate attack. In his off-hand he still held the jagged bottom half of the shattered axe handle which he stabbed upwards into Forglug's midsection. Still rising to his feet Ma-Gur easily sidestepped the other orc's interrupted swing and with his right hand used his broken battleaxe to sever Forgulg's right arm at the shoulder. The combination of sudden wounds bowled the unfortunate orc over, his mangled form spinning from the blow as the toppled down.

Nearly losing consciousness from his wounds and the loss of blood Ma-Gur lost his own footing and fell to one knee. There was a moment of silence as Ma-Gur bowed his head, then a gurgling howl sounded as the young orc looked up in alarm.

Forglug has somehow managed to get to his feet and was charging the kneeling Ma-Gur with sword held aloft with is remaining arm. With a pained groan Ma-Gur sprang to his feet and met the charge. His hand shot out to grasp Forglug's descending wrist, stopping short the devastating blow. Without hesitating, Ma-Gur buried his axe in Forglug's neck, nearly severing the stout orc's head from his shoulders. Forglug immediately fell to his knees as Ma-Gur struck his neck again, this time decapitating him.

The arena was silent for a moment as all watched the blood pump out from Forglug's savaged corpse. Ma-Gur, with the battle-lust still burning brightly in his eyes, raised his bloodied arms to the sky and roared. It felt so good! He drew a breath and roared again, this time his voice was joined by the deep-throated growls of his fellow survivors.

Their response caught his attention, and with a wicked grin he turned and began to advance menacingly towards the nearest youngling. The growls died in their throats as the other orcs stopped in their surprise at this new happening. Ma-Gur and the youngling raised their weapons as if they were going to fight. A look of resignation and bloodlust was on the face of the youngling, who knew he was no match for this approaching monster yet was determined to fight to the last. As they neared each other a powerful voice filled the air, stopped them in their tracks, though their eyes still betrayed barely contained violence.

"Enough!" Bellowed the Ghalik as he thumped the butt of his war axe on the ground at his feet.

"Only the unworthy die today," he commanded, "You thirty younglings are the survivors. The Blooded! You have proven yourselves in battle and are now worthy of the tattoos you bear. Now it is your duty to remember this day, now that you have learned this is what makes you Angir. Let us return home as victors."

The Ghalik motioned for the warriors to restack their weapons as they filed out of the arena and back down the mountain. The haphazard pile of killing implements increased as Ghalik drew a shiny new mace from his belt and threw it on the stack before he turned to go. The weapons grew cold in the mountain wastes, waiting until spilt blood warmed them again.

Chapter 2

The crude boats glided silently across the icy surface of the slow moving river. The thin layer of frost gave way as the thin crafts made their way. These were neither the sleek canoes of the elves nor the strong flatboats of men and dwarf. The roughness of their arrow shaped design and the haphazard style of the craftsmanship gave away their orcish origins. Despite their primitive design they were good vessels, stronger, but slower than elf craft and faster yet not as strong as the ships of man and dwarf. Each one was designed to hold four occupants. The orcs at either end of the boat did the paddling while the two in the middle held spears at the ready, in case of an opportunity to attack or the need to defend.

In this manner, several score of such vessels made their way down river. A few days down the river lay a port town of men. In ages past, the town had been larger and relatively undefended, but as the strength, numbers, and ambitions of the nearby Angir grew the townspeople felt the pressure to build. Now the town of nearly four hundred people conducted its affairs within the protection of high walls and mercenary guardsmen. So far the building of fortifications and the garrison of mercenaries had fought off the small orc raids.

Little did they know that Ghalik of the Angir had been biding his time, holding off the main assault for reasons far more sinister than fear of walls or hired swords. He had been planning this raid for sometime now.

He had a fresh crop of young warriors in need of their first taste of manflesh. They were eager to prove themselves, and Ghalik knew that if he did not direct their bloodlust towards real enemies they would turn on each other. Raiding has been slowing down considerably in the last few years anyway. Towns were either being abandoned or becoming impregnable. It wasn't that Ghalik or the Angir feared to lay siege to these fortified cities, it was that the Angir were few in number compared to the number of towns and their full compliments of sellswords and militiamen. Being such a small tribe was a difficult thing, especially considering the tribe's ancient custom of the Blooding. Siege required vast amounts of resources and large numbers of troops. Raiding, however, was the perfect method of warfare for the orcs of the Angir. As such, they were masters of hit and run assaults and were crack shock troops. To them, siege warfare was the lowest form of combat.

The Angir were going to have to expand, thought the Ghalik as he sat in his boat, the great waraxe of his predecessor lying across his lap. Perhaps they could overthrow the orcish clans in the south, who were large in number and had many strong women for childbearing. At this Ghalik began to think of his own childbearer. A great and bloated creature. He smiled as he pictured her resting her girth upon the mats and pillows that adorned her part of the Motherhut. Surely by now all of the women would be awake, gorging themselves on whatever food was brought to them by their youngling servants. After all, for most of their pampered lives they were eating for seven to ten.

The Ghalik was the only orc with a woman all his own. While he had the privilege of breeding with her and choosing his heir from his own litters, all other Angir males had to constantly compete for breeding rights. The women would only deign to breed with the strongest and mightiest orcs of the tribe. So it was with most orc tribes ensuring that the race as a whole moved ever closer to supremacy.

Ma-Gur also thought of these things as he paddled the boat steadily onwards. Last night he'd had his first mating experience, his bruises from the encounter still fresh and sore. Having had such an impressive Blooding rite, Ma-Gur had been chosen by one of the younger women to share her bed. So after a few days of healing his wounds he had gone inside the Motherhut.

Orcish women are violent and passionate creatures, often quite dominant during the act of love. Many a tale was told around the campfires of mighty orc warriors being "savaged" by their women. Laughter and a few knowing looks usually accompanied such stories.

A harsh whisper tore Ghalik from his reverie and Ma-Gur from his bruises. The raiding party had neared the fortified village. The glow from the sentry's torches could be seen in the distance. The raiding party quietly grouped their boats together, silently moving towards the dock en masse.

As they neared the docks, the orcs steered their boats towards the dockside shore. Once they reached more shallow water they disembarked their vessels, sliding silently into the shoulder deep water. It was frigid in temperature yet no warrior flinched or complained. They pushed their boats ashore then returned to the shoulder depth shallows. They waded towards the docks as their hot fetid breath hung in clouds all about them.

The docks were built to service the main town gate. All of the loading platforms had walkways across the shallows and right up to the main gate. A handful of sentries were posted at the docks and two guarded the main gate. None of the sentries noticed as the orc raiding party waded towards the gate through the water right underneath them. The sentries had no worry that such a thing would be attempted. No man could stay in that water for more than a few moments without risk of freezing to death, but these were not men.

At a gesture from Ghalik, the main group of orcs continued towards the gate while Ma-Gur and four of his blood brothers stayed behind. Their duty was to disable the group of sentries on the docks as the main force brought down the gate. The young orc had no idea how the wizard was going to open the gate, but Ma-Gur did know exactly what to do about the sentries.

He gestured to each orc indicating where he wanted them and what they should do. It was an advantage of the orc race that so much information could be communicated without words. Soon each orc nodded in turn and set about his task.

The orcs spread out underneath the dock. Then the orcs grasped the support beams and each one began to climb up a different beam. Their claw like fingernails and bulging muscles allowed them to climb stealthily upwards with relative ease. As they reached the top the orcs peered out onto the surface of the docking platforms.

There were four sentries armed with crossbows walking a lazy beat around the docking area, totally unaware of the looming threat. Ma-Gur ducked back under the dock to peer into the darkness towards the underside of the platform nearest the gate. With his orcish night sight he saw the hulking forms of Ghalik and his older, more experienced warriors right next to the gate. Ghalik noticed Ma-Gur's inquisitive look and nodded back. Ma-Gur gave his four comrades an affirmative nod and began to climb.

As the sentries walked their beat one of them heard a scraping noise. He turned on his heel, his crossbow held before him, but say only the empty edge of the dock. Suddenly, just as he relaxed and lowered his weapon, an especially nasty looking creature with a white tattooed face rose up from its perch upon the support beam. Before the guard could react it hurled a wickedly barbed spear straight into his chest.

Hearing the impact of metal and flesh the other guards turned towards the sound. As they did, three other orcs launched themselves onto the platform hurling spears as they came. Two of the guards went down without a word, their surprise melting away as they collapsed with spears in their chests. The third sentry was faster than the others and with his off hand managed to deflect the spear away from his chest and into his leg. Biting back the pain as he fell to one knee. The wounded guard aimed his crossbow and fired. The arrow caught one of the orcs in the throat, which stumbled back and fell into the water as he gurgled and choked. The sentry drew his sword to defend himself, but died instantly when Ma-Gur's sword splint his skull as the orc came running up from behind.

Once Ghalik nodded for Ma-Gur to begin the assault, the ugly wizard had waved his hand at the two warriors nearest him, gesturing for them to kill the two gate guards. The two experienced warriors sprang into action, each one taking a different side of the dock. They moved quietly and quickly as they waded out of the water and crept towards the two gate guards. When the attention of the sentries was distracted as the battle on the docks began, the two orcs made their move.

Just as the sentries looked up to witness the ambush on the docks, the two orcs came at them from both sides. The guard on the left never saw them coming, dying soundlessly as the orcish mace crushed his helmeted head. The guard on the right was given a few moments to react due to the longer climb forced upon the other ambushing orc. He managed to bring his spear into a defensive position and brace for the attack. The orc rushed furiously towards him brandishing a large cleaver with both hands. The oncoming orc leveled a powerful blow at the guardsman, who just managed to duck out of the way, the cleaver making sparks fly as it chipped off a piece of the stone walkway. The guardsman stepped foreword with a counter strike, plunging his spear into the enemy's guts.

To his horrifying surprise the orc did not go down, in fact, with an intensified fury it pushed itself down the shaft of the spear. To late the guardsman realized his mistake, as the orc further impaled itself it was drawing closer to the man holding the weapon. The guard tried to let loose of the weapon and flee, but before he could, the berserker orc dispatched him with its cleaver.

The guard's body crumpled to the ground as the wounded orc bent over, supporting its weight upon its upturned cleaver. Ghalik and the others were making their way up to the gate, they were quickly joined by Ma-Gur and his remaining ambush party.

"Hold him," Ghalik commanded as he moved closer to the wounded orc. As the old wizard rummaged in his belt pouch the older warriors moved to support and brace the wounded orc. Many of them had seen what was about to happen and tensed, the younger warriors looked on in wonder.

Ghalik pulled from his pouch a small sack, which appeared to be full of some kind of powder. The wizard walked up to the wounded orc and drew forth a fistful of a glowing green dust like substance. He held it aloft and spoke in the broken syllables of magic, as he did the glow of the green dust faded. Then he began to smear the powder all around the wound until it was completely covered. He took a quick step back and broke off the shaft of the spear, leaving the point securely embedded in the wound.

The old wizard quickly stepped back and nodded at the warriors holding the wounded orc, who tightened their grip in anticipation of what they seemed to know was coming. Ghalik gestured towards the rest of his forces.

"Split into two groups, one on the left and one on the right," barked Ghalik as he unshouldered his waraxe, hefting its weight like a familiar friend, "Lorak will take the center."

At this the older warriors cast a wary glance towards the wounded orc, Lorak, who was now shaking uncontrollably. Only the brute strength of the others holding him down kept the orc from convulsing so hard he injured himself. The younger warriors hesitated in curiosity of the wounded orc plight, but were quickly jostled into formation by the older warriors.

The two groups of orcs stood in loose clusters on their respective sides of the gate. While orcs were not known for making uniform or complex battle formations, they did have a grasp of strategy. The primary reason for their seemingly simple organization was that once the fighting began each individual orc would basically do as he pleased, so formations tended to crumble into seething tides of berserkers.

Ghalik knew this, and he used it to his advantage. Once inside the town everyone would go their own way, each seeking his own glory. Thus, the battle would spread quickly throughout the area as the orcs jockeyed for position. Yet Ghalik also knew that the older orcs now feared Lorak, and that fear would spread to the younger warriors. Fear would keep everyone in formation long enough for his plan to work and bring victory to all.

Ghalik stopped close to the city gate, its metal hinges and sturdy wooden planks barring the way of the would-be invaders. He began to sway back and forth as if in a trance, his eyes closed as he whispered in the maddening language of orcish magic. He began to flex his arms and heft the axe as if he were going to strike the gate. Then he would let the waraxe fall slack again. He repeated the process over and over again, each time reaching a higher crescendo.

Ma-Gur looked at Ghalik with an intense mixture of fear and admiration. He knew that Ghalik was the oldest orc Angir, some said the oldest orc alive. There were legends of his exploits told to Angir children and songs of his glory sung over the burning villages of the enemy. For Ma-Gur it was like taking part in a legend, as if just by being a witness to the evening's events were enough to include him.

Then he felt a tingling sensation of the back of his neck. A strange glow was being emitted from the waraxe in Ghalik's hands. It was as if the very air around the murmuring wizard was shimmering and pregnant with powerful energies. Ma-Gur felt as if he too was in a deep trance as he watched the wizard craft his spell.

Suddenly Ma-Gur's attention was torn from the Ghalik by a low rumble that seemed to come from everywhere at once. He turned to investigate, his eyes falling upon the wounded Lorak. The two warriors who were holding him down had backed away, leaving the wounded orc kneeling alone. As he stared in wonder, Lorak's head shot up. His now bright red eyes boring right into Ma-Gur's very soul. Even as those eyes seemed to burn him, the pupils emitting wisps of red smoke which could not be natural. As they stared at each other, Lorak's eyes sent a message that Ma-Gur could not help but to receive. This was no longer an orc, but death made manifest. The horrible truth struck him as he turned away, fear and elation threatening to pull him apart.

When he turned back he could see that Ghalik appeared to have completed his ritual, and was now standing before the gate with his feet planted and his shimmering axe held high. The shouts of the guards on the other side of the gate could be heard, drawn no doubt by the Ghalik's incessant bellowing. The orc horde tensed as Ghalik slammed the blazing waraxe against the sturdy gate. The blast of energy was amazing as the enchanted weapon hit home. The entire gate blew apart with the sound of a thunderclap, all of the splintered wood and twisted metal bursting into flames as they flew in all directions.

The older orcs paused a moment before rushing to battle, causing the younger warriors to look about in confusion. Then an earth-shaking roar sounded from behind them. Some of the younger orcs turned to witness Lorak, or more precisely something that used to be Lorak, launch itself from its crouched position towards the smoldering gate. It still bore Lorak's face, though its body had almost doubled in size and strength. Its nails had turned to claws and its lower teeth into tusks. Even the Ghalik hurried out of its way as it lopped past, easily covering the distance in a few strides.

Most of the guards who had gathered at the gate were dead or stunned and offered no resistance as the Lorak creature strode past them, its hungry gaze falling upon the town as alarms were raised an the townspeople began to wake. As its hulking form disappeared down the main street of town the two orcish forces moved in on either side. Now Ghalik's plan went into action. As he had hoped, one of his warriors had been mortally wounded during the ambush, giving him a body into which he could summon the tribe's killing spirit, the Gor-Angir. Now he wouldn't have to sacrifice one of the orcs himself. Leadership wasn't always about brute force alone. Fear of the Gor-Angir would keep the two raiding parties on separate sides of the city. The killing spirit would undoubtedly perish, but it would throw into chaos what defenses this port town could muster, leaving the orcs free to pillage the town without being set upon by large groups of organized troops. Ghalik smiled, this was shaping up to be a rather enjoyable evening.

The two groups of orcs headed in their respective directions, organized in that they did not stray towards the central street but otherwise moving as a seething horde of muscle and steel. The defenseless gate guards were the first to die, lying in helpless heaps as the orcs butchered them without breaking stride. Soon the gate complex was empty save for the soft moans of the dying and the sounds of battle coming from inside the town as the orc menace spread out to plunder and kill.

Ma-Gur stepped out into the main street, the smoldering creak of the blasted gateway filling the air as a wind blew up from the shore. The young orc barely noticed the icy breeze as he stare down the main street of town, after Lorak, or the Gor-Angir as Ghalik had told them. They were all to stay out of its path, skirting the edges so that the town's defenders would be occupied with dispatching the berserk monster and not be able to mount a formidable resistance as the night wore on. Ghalik had gone with one of the groups, even the mighty wizard shied away from the killing spirit.

But they had not gazed into its eyes, thought Ma-Gur. They did not see the truth about what Lorak had become. Those eyes said, "let the world burn," so honest and so brutal. The young orc was mystified, desiring nothing more greatly than to witness the Gor-Angir in action. He wanted to see what it was capable of, and in many ways, what he was capable of in comparison. Ma-Gur tightened his grip on the bloody sword in his hand, slung his shield onto his arm, and took his first steps down the town's main street.

It seemed to him as if he had been creeping along forever. All about him were burning buildings and corpses of the slain. Most of them were townsfolk, mostly women and children. Awakened from their beds no doubt. Judging from the sorts of wounds on the bodies, Ma-Gur found that he was not only able to track the progress of the Gor-Angir, but could move at speed because of how messy and obvious the killing spirit's victims were. Bodies rent to pieces were not the work of fast moving raiders with blades, but by the taloned hands of a creature from beyond the pale.

He carefully picked his way along as possible, avoiding the rampaging orcs as they glutted themselves on the vulnerable city and its inhabitants. As the young orc quickened his pace an old woman ran around the corner in panic. Almost before he realized what he was doing he had rammed his meaty fist into her jaw, snapping her head back and breaking her neck. The poor woman's knees buckled and she collapsed as Ma-Gur continued on his way without further pause.

His blood screamed with battle-lust as he heard the freakish bellowing of the killing spirit just up ahead. He broke into a dead run uphill towards what appeared to be the town square. The sounds of intense fighting could be heard coming from the square. Ma-Gur slowed his pace and peered out into the square from behind a corner.

His eyes widened at what he saw. The Gor-Angir was covered from head to foot in wounds, arrows, and broken spear tips. It was visibly weakened and appeared to be losing much of its power. Yet strewn all about the square were the broken bodies of more than a dozen men at arms and pikemen. There was still that same number standing, fighting a desperate battle with the monster.

Their strategy was simple, after losing half of their number so quickly simple tactics were all that remained for the hard-pressed survivors. They had surrounded the creature and were barely managing to keep it at bay with the combined might of their spears. As Ma-Gur watched several archers came from the vantage points of doorways and alleys to get closer to the beast for easier shots.

The young orc suddenly realized that if nothing was done the Gor-Angir was about to perish. Ma-Gur realized that the creature was meant to die, but it seemed almost an affront to the killing spirit for it to die not in battle, but pin cushioned by the arrows of cowards. Summoning up all his fury and courage Ma-Gur rushed out from his hiding place.

He kept his wits about him, and instead of uttering a battle cry he allowed the crunching sound of the nearest pikeman's head speak for him. It was only when the eyes of all the men went to him, as well as those of the Gor-Angir, that he realized how foolish he had been.

With a bestial roar the Gor-Angir lashed out and caved in the chest of a nearby man at arms. Then, with surprising agility for such a wounded and hulking creature, it spun on its heel to avoid the sword swipe of another man at arms. With a furious howl it raked its talons across the man's midsection, spilling his steaming guts into the cold streets.

Ma-Gur tore his attention away from the creature as he suddenly found every bit of sword and shield training he had ever received tested by two men at arms intent on ending his life. He backed towards the center of the square as he gave ground to his attackers. He took a chance move and allowed a strike past his guard, catching the oncoming blade at the last moment in the shield's sword-breaking grove. His luck held as he turned the shield aside, both breaking the blade and leaving the man at arms unable to parry the blow that separated his head from his shoulders.

Before the young orc could recover from his strike the other man at arms closed in for a vicious stab at his midsection. Ma-Gur did not try to parry the attack, but instead closed distance himself and twisted his body away from the blow. The sharp blade passed right by as Ma-Gur pirouetted and brought his shield around to bash in the back of the human's skull. Ma-Gur smiled savagely at the sound of breaking bone and crushed metal as the man at arms flew forwards and to the ground.

His reverie was interrupted by a deep rumbling sound with filled him with its menace. He turned towards the source of the sounds and his blood run cold as he found himself face to face with the Gor-Angir. It paused for a moment, the din of battle seeming to melt away for that one instant that the two locked eyes.

Ma-Gur knew he was about to die. The look in the killing spirit's eyes made it plain enough. He suddenly shook his head violently, clearing away the lethargy that the maddening gaze had set upon him. The Gor-Angir's keen senses picked up on Ma-Gur's return to awareness, it roared in its unslakeable bloodlust as it dashed towards the young orc.

All the while the two creatures had been staring each other down the human warriors had not been idle. They had reformed their shattered circle and were closing in for the kill, the heads of their pikes glittering in the firelight.

Ma-Gur jumped back away from the killing spirit, and was about to turn and run when a sudden pain in his shoulder flooded his perception. *Maybe the spell was real after all,* he thought as he reached up to grasp the spear point that was protruding from underneath his left collarbone. As an orc he was relatively capable of withstanding pain, yet as a flesh and blood creature he realized that he was not without his limits.

The Gor-Angir had nearly reached the young orc as Ma-Gur spun on his heel to face the spearman. In the process of turning around Ma-Gur was able to break the shaft of the spear, thus regaining control over his movements. As the human reeled in surprise the orc roughly grabbed the man underneath the armpits, and with a desperate snarl turned and hurled him towards the oncoming monster.

The killing spirit was distracted by the spearman flying through the air towards it. Though only for a moment as it swatted the poor man savagely in mid-air as if it were batting away meddlesome insects. Ma-Gur gaped in disbelief as the power and strength of the creature, even as it bore down on him, surely to end his life.

Again Ma-Gur forced him to snap out of the mental stasis that the presence of the creature seemed to cause. He turned once more to flee only to find his way barred by several of the surviving pikemen. Ma-Gur put on a burst of speed as he let out a war cry and raised his sword in a suicidal charge. The pikemen resolutely set their weapons to meet his charge, their faces masks of determination tinged with a fear of not only Ma-Gur, but also the abomination that swept along just behind the muscular young orc.

As the distance between Ma-Gur and the sharp points of the human's pikes shortened the Gor-Angir was beginning to stretch out its massive taloned hands. At the last instant Ma-Gur lowered his sword and ducked into a roll, his body careening across the ground in a somersault and through the legs of the center pikeman. The orc's momentum carried him through the pikemen's line, knocking the luckless human to the ground. Ma-Gur rose from his tumble at a dead run, making for the raised edge of the town square. If he could just clear the wall he would be able to escape the monster, perhaps even survive to join his blood brothers in battle elsewhere.

The fallen pikeman rose to his knees just in time to see the taloned hand that swooped down to rend his throat. The other two humans made a valiant attempt to save their comrade. One took a step forward and plunged his weapon's point deep into the creature's thigh. While he was attacking the other warrior made a jab at the Gor-Angir's misshapen skull.

The enraged killing spirit lashed out with its talons, and the warrior striking at its head disappeared in a spray of blood and bone. The warrior who had managed to wound it found himself lifted up brutally by the jaw. He was unconscious from the pressure of the creature's grip almost instantly, so did not notice as his neck snapped as his body was flung through the air.

Ma-Gur reached the wall in a panic. He knew the thing was behind him, and it did not sound like the spearmen had stalled it for very long. He dared not look back however, preferring to keep his eyes on the wall that would help him survive this mess. The young orc barely paused to check what was on the other side or how far the drop was as he vaulted the high wall.

In mid-air he was struck with the corpse of a human warrior, the blow knocking him nearly senseless. He crumpled to the ground after a short fall, which hurt only because he failed to land his feet.

The Gor-Angir was preparing to leap off the wall after the young orc when several arrows thudded into its back. It turned quickly to meet the new threat, and found itself faced with half a dozen human warriors, battered but not broken, and charged.

Ma-Gur quickly climbed to his feet. The blow from the corpse had winded him, but not enough to cool the fires of fear. He snatched up his sword and fled deeper into the village.

For many long hours the town burned. The cold night was warmed by the blazing of fire and the steam of spilt blood. Many dramas and tragedies were played out under the unblinking gaze of the stars. It was a long time before the clash of steel ceased or the keening of the wounded and grieving grew silent.

As the first light of dawn crept over the mountains the kiss of the sun fell upon a burned husk of a town, a shadow of what it once was. Where there were once longhouses and meadhalls there were smoldering ruins and piles of ash. Where there were once people conducting their morning business now there were only orcs.

They moved silently about the dead city, plundering the area for what booty could be salvaged. Most of them had been too intent upon battle and murder to concern themselves with wealth. So it was with their kind, setting fire to the corpses of both man and orc, even the mutilated corpse of the Gor-Angir after it had finally fallen to the desperate might of the defenders. As dawn became morning the orcs waded back to their boats and set off for home. The older warriors were stoic and proud, Ghalik had once again delivered the enemy into their hands, another victory for the living legend. The younger warriors acted as if in a daze, still intoxicated by the rush of battle and pain.

Ma-Gur sat apart from the others, his newfound insights still smoldering within him. Ghalik watched the younger orc with an appraising eye. The youngling had disobeyed him, but the haunted look in the warrior's eyes told Ghalik that this new knowledge was punishment enough. The orcs set out up river to return home as the carrion that circled the town descended into theirs.

Chapter 3

The rough-cut boats made their way slowly up the river, the orc's powerful strokes inching the boats along against the current. The run off from the morning melting had swollen the river, and the calm frozen river of night had become a treacherous afternoon ice floe. However, the orcs of the Angir were capable oarsmen and for nearly two days managed to skillfully avoid being sunk by the fast moving ice chunks.

Since going up river was a much slower process the sun was almost at its height on the third day before the raiding party was near enough to home to see the smoke. It was rising up through the trees in several places, white and soft wisps quietly billowing upwards into the sky. Ghalik did not need to tell the group to pick up speed, at the sight of the smoke the orcs were already dipping their oars at a superhuman pace.

They came around the bend in the river with spears poised, ready to repel any attackers whom sought to blindside them. On the beach there were many track and boat impressions on the coarse beach. The orcs were out of their boats and splashing ashore as they drew weapons and readied shields. After a moment Okada, the closest thing the Angir had to a scout, ran up to Ghalik to make his report.

"It appears that a force of men landed here and moved up the trail towards home. From the freshness of the tracks I would say that they arrived only shortly after we began our journey back upriver," reported the breathless ranger.

"Did they return here, or to they await us in the village?" Ghalik questioned as he absently fingered his waraxe.

"I believe they came back this way. The tracks indicate that they came back down the path and left with their boats. Whatever happened here, we are too late," explained Okada as he looked down.

Ghalik grunted derisively at Okada's display of emotion, this was no time to grieve. The old wizard unslung his waraxe and gave a hand signal to the waiting warriors, indicating that it was time to move in. The horde, which had only suffered minimal casualties in the raid, moved up the trail silently. Everyone moved with a quiet urgency, their dread of what the smoke most likely meant was hard to mask.

The horde of warriors poured out of the forest and into the village, all secretly hoping that what lie before them would shimmer and disappear like a forgotten dream. They did not. Fires still burned and the smell of death was quite pungent and fresh. Ghalik ordered the group to spread out by clinching his fist then opening it again quickly, splaying out his fingers to symbolize his command. The orc warriors did as they were told and moved into the burning village.

Ma-Gur ended up stalking into the village next to Okada, the two orcs exchanging a grim nod as they tightened their grip on their weapons and advanced. They moved in close to the winter larders, the smell of burnt flesh clinging to their nostrils. The two orcs reached the building, its primary structure of mud and sticks totally burned away to reveal the still burning hardwood support beams. All of the food and cooking supplies that the Angir had stocked to see them through the winter lie in burnt heaps of melted fat and stinking ash.

As they stood in silent shock at the entrance to the burnt shell of the building they heard a small cry. Both immediately beared their weapons and prepared to fight, but no attack came. Again they heard the cry, this time the two orcs could tell where it was coming from.

"The children's warren," gasped Okada as he took off at a run towards a low ceilinged building near the ruined larder.

Ma-Gur quickly followed, but the larger orc had difficulty keep up with the smaller and faster scout. The two orcs reached the building just as three other warriors who had also heard the call arrived as well. With the quiet understanding so common to their race the five orcs spread out to surround the collapsed building. Once in position they converged on the center as they again heard the cry.

Ma-Gur and another warrior reached the source of the sound, which was coming from underneath a pile of collapsed mud wall that was being held down by a broken support beam. Ma-Gur and the warrior strained their muscles as they lifted the massive wooden beam. Okada and the other two orcs quickly began digging away the crumpled pieces of the wall as they heard the cry again.

They found a young orcish boy who had been pinned down underneath the crumbling wall. He was crying because it appeared that his leg was broken. With firmly set jaws the five warriors paused a moment to look at the boy. Unfathomable expressions played out over their faces, and then left as quickly as they came as their faces hardened once more. Okada reached out to hold the boy, firmly bracing him as another warrior grasped the boy's broken leg. There was a moment of silence, then it was broken by a loud cracking noise and the boy's yelp of pain as the orc set the bone.

The five warriors emerged from the smoke. Ma-Gur was carrying the boy, whose small arms were wrapped tightly around the big orc's stout neck. The rest of the assembled orcs watched without comment, knowing better than to ask about the other children. Yet even the boy was only meant to live a short time. For as Ma-Gur walked on the boy's arms fell slack, the shock of his leg and massive internal injuries just too much for his young body. The large warrior gently laid the body upon the ground, and walked on with downcast eyes.

The bodies of the small handful of orc warriors chosen to be left behind to defend the village lay scattered about the entrance of the settlement. Their bodies were hacked and bloody, many of them were riddled with strangely beautiful arrows. There was blood on a few of their weapons, which meant that at least they hadn't died alone.

One of the living orc warriors yanked an arrow from a body and held it out to Okada to examine. The scout looked at it for a moment, then broke the arrow in his hand in disgust.

"Elves," he spat as he threw the pieces at the torn ground.

"And men," stated an orc who came out of the smoke with a few other warriors behind him. Over his shoulder was a body, which he unceremoniously dumped on the ground.

It was the corpse of a human male, a warrior by his armor. It appeared that before his body was buried and partially burned that he had worn a white surcoat. A well-known symbol of the men of Iithsul, religious zealots from a country far to the south.

"What are templars doing this far north?" asked one of the warriors.

"They most likely came at the behest of the Dalarns. Some of them escaped last spring when we sacked the city. Those limp-wristed pixie loving elves were probably scouts or something for the templars," cursed another orc.

"Who were likely the only people who would aid the Dalarn survivors,"

Okada mused as he looked at the destruction surrounding them.

"I knew we should have run them down when we had the chance, too busy setting fire to the place," grumbled one of the orcs. His comment was answered by a handful of snorts and grunts, the closest expressions to laughter that most orcs made once reaching adulthood.

The group of warriors were interrupted from their subdued reverie as they heard the heavy footfalls of the majority of the horde tromping by. The remaining orcs quickly fell into step with the rest as they moved towards the back of the village.

What used to be the grandest, by orcish standards, building in the village was nothing more than a smoking heap. The Motherhut, living quarters for all the females of the Angir, had been completely destroyed. Even the massive hardwood timbers had been pulled from the ground. The hacked and charred bodies of the large females lay strewn about the area, and some could be seen partially buried under the smoldering debris.

The entirety of the orc warriors had congregated around the demolished structure. Not a sound stirred the silence that had descended upon the area. The orcs looked upon their slain women with numb acceptance. Death in battle was no stranger, but the sort of annihilation that faced them was beyond their experience. No one pointed out the obvious, that no more children would be born of an Angir mother. Certainly other mothers could be found, but the Angir bloodline, so ancient and strong, was now doomed to fade.

Ghalik, who had been standing silently next to the savaged body of his exclusive female, lifted his head to look at the assembled warriors. It was as if he somehow sensed the sudden decline in moral, a loss of will and might. He understood their grief and loss, perhaps more than they did themselves. For seven hundred years she had belonged to him and him to her, now so much discarded meat. He set his jaw firmly as he made his decision to carry on, it was that simple. He took a step towards the assembled orcs and began to speak.

"Warriors of the Angir, I know what you are feeling right now. We have been struck a mighty blow this day. One from which we will never recover. A mortal wound that will in the passing of time seal our doom. When the last of us dies, the true Angir will be no more," intoned Ghalik as he paced like a caged animal.

"Oh yes we could take wives from other tribes. Strange women could bear our children and raise our families, but they would not be Angir. We have been dealt our death blow today," he uttered as he suddenly pointed at

Ma-Gur, "You. What do we do when a warrior is dealt a horrible wound, but does not die?"

Ma-Gur almost balked at the dangerous sparkle in the old wizard's eyes, then he realized what the Ghalik was implying. The thought set his heart to racing.

"We pack his wound with magic and summon into him the killing spirit of our tribe," stated the young orc, pride and fear making his voice rumble. At his words the assembled orcs opened their mouths in shock.

"The Gor-Angir," hissed Ghalik as he smiled wickedly, "Are we not wounded warriors? Are not our wounds packed with the ashes of our dying tribe? The mothers are gone, and all that remains are we the fighters. What else can we be except killing spirits? We are the Gor-Angir. Made by our enemies so that our vengeance will know no bounds!"

His speech was answered by the deep rumbling howls of the horde. Ghalik joined them in their primal scream, venting their rage and sorrow at the impassive skies above. Generations later woodsmen and trappers brave and foolish enough to work the frozen mountains still tell stories about the day the mountains raised their voices to the gods. Angered that men were allowed to pass upon their snow-covered slopes.

Chapter 4

The old wizard carefully stirred the last of the glowing green powder into the warped and fire blackened pot he had discovered in the wreckage of the village's larder. While he was busy mixing the powder the rest of the orcs were scavenging what they could from the desolate area. Very little useful items had been spared, it was as if the enemy had known the warriors would return and have to face the winter without equipment or supplies. The relatively empty handed warrior began to congregate around Ghalik as they returned from their fruitless searches.

"We will never catch them if we do not give ourselves some kind of advantage," stated the wizard as he finally finished mixing and stood up to face the now fully assembled horde.

"The wound is in our hearts, so we will drink this potion to get the magic inside us," continued Ghalik as he poured the contents of the pot into the large waterskin he carried at his side. While he did this the watching orcs grumbled to themselves, knowing full well what the powder could do and questioning the purpose of taking such a risk. Ghalik sensed the derision, so took a quick drink from the skin. The orcs backed up a step in fear and surprise at the breaking of an ancient taboo. Ghalik turned and walked towards them.

"Everyone must drink. Take this potion and you will be able to have your revenge. You won't become monsters, there is to little magic for it to happen to us all. But what you do take will give you the power to catch our enemies, no matter what lead they have on us," Ghalik bellowed as he looked at the orcs gathered around him, "Who has the courage to become the Gor-Angir, and take the fight to those foolish men?"

Ma-Gur stepped forward. He did not quite know why, but something in the eyes of the monster last night seemed to drive him to step up. The young orc walked up to Ghalik and held out his hand. Ghalik gave a twisted grin and handed the skin to Ma-Gur. The young warrior put the skin to his lips and poured a small measure into his mouth. The taste of it was like a strong acid, bitter and corrosive as it carried the ancient magic deep into his body.

Ma-Gur stepped aside as the next orc moved to take his place, and one by one the entire horde each took their swallow of bitter potion. The orcs then stood silently, waiting for Ghalik to speak.

The old wizard looked around himself at the assembled force, his mind on fire with the violent magic in his belly. He slung his axe on to his back and began walking back down to the shore.

"We must cross the river as soon as we can. The magic works quickly, and we will soon need to be on the move. Should we tarry the magic will make us end up killing each other. Our only option is to run, and keep running 'til we find the enemy. You will not stop. You will not tire. They will be ours before dusk tomorrow," he commanded as the orcs loaded themselves into the boats and began crossing the narrow river.

Once they reached the other side the orc piled out of the boats. Their eyes were slowly turning red, and everyone felt the berserker rush signaling that the spell was beginning to take effect. Okada pointed to a quite visible path, the underbrush and dirt torn and disheveled. The enemy had not bothered to cover their tracks, so sure that no one would give chase much less catch them.

All of the orcs present could tell that the enemy had horses and carts, so would cover ground very quickly. The men also had nearly three full days lead on the horde. Yet as the Gor-Angir began to manifest, the orcs did not feel overwhelmed. Instead they felt eager for the chase, the rush of the hunt soon overcame them and they took off down the trail.

The horde moved quickly along the trail left by the enemy. They ran at top speeds, their seemingly tireless bodies eating up the miles as the day wore on. They were so enmeshed with the Gor-Angir that they did not notice the passing of time or the subtle changes in the landscape. By nightfall the orcs had left the ice capped mountains and were moving through the evergreen forests that lay at the base of the mountain and beyond.

A thunderstorm rolled down the mountain and poured itself out onto the forest below. Oblivious to the cold or the wet, the orcs continued on, their feet pounding through the mud as they chased their quarry. As the sun rose over the forest the orcs were still running unceasingly down the trail. Their eyes were a burning red and their muscles seemed to have grown during the night. Their only thoughts were those of blood and death, so intent upon their goal that they did not feel fatigue or hunger. The trees were thinning as morning became afternoon, still they did not give up the chase as they emerged onto open tundra. The cold plains rising to meet their feet as they continued on.

The elves had ranged a small distance ahead of the main body of the small army. They carefully picked their way along the small trail, their bows ready and arrows knocked. They were disgusted with the arrogance and haughtiness of the templars. These men felt that because their High King had charged them with wiping out an orc tribe that they were masters of the realm. Victory always had made men prideful they thought, add on top of that religious justification and one ended up with spectacularly superior feeling bullies. Still, the elves begrudgingly respected the martial prowess and dedication of these men. They heeded the cries of the Dalarn when no others had, calling a general crusade against all of the old races, so perhaps their need to do good offset their somewhat boorish personalities.

The elves continued moving until, almost as one, the dozen elves stopped dead in their tracks. The knights and carts behind them slowed.

"There is something on the wind," uttered one of the elves as he motioned for the knights to keep moving, "A foul energy comes our way. We must hasten away."

"We'll not run from battle my friend. Better to meet it head on than be stabbed in the back. Though we will heed you for now, I trust your judgment even if I disagree with your perceptions of valor," spoke the lead knight as he gave the signal to move out.

The small army returned to its journey, plodding along on their carts and armored horses. This was not a caravan designed to cover ground quickly, yet could still easily outpace anyone on foot. Or so it was assumed. The mounted knights were not ignoring the elf's warnings however, and kept a wary eye on the woods about them. Likely as not, the only menace in these woods would be the goblin clans, most of whom had been wiped out by other crusading armies. Goblins were much shorter than men or orcs, though they shared a similar lust for death and plunder. However, unlike the tendency towards raiding and open combat of the orcs, goblins were a skittish race more suited to ambush and murders in the night. Still, thought most of the knights, even goblins could be dangerous if constant vigilance was not maintained.

The feeling of danger and foreboding began to prick the minds of the elves, like a little thorn of fear stabbing at their resolve. With the exchange of a few meaningful glances the elves made clear to each other that all of them sensed trouble coming. Without a word they split into two groups and disappeared into the surrounding forest. It was long moments before the knights and their retainers noticed their disappearance. With a gesture of his hand the knight's leader ordered a halt. The years of training in knighthood had an immediate effect, as the knights instinctively formed a circle around the wagons.

The elves backtracked along the edges of the trail, their hearts beating madly as their almost supernaturally keen senses picked up on the palpable danger moving towards them. They silently emerged onto the trail as they crested the hill. Suddenly they were assaulted by a petrifying wave of fear as they looked into the valley below.

A horde of orcs with blazing red eyes and bright white tattoos were scaling the hill, the first of their number already closing distance to engage. The elves were a tall and slender race thought to be the descendants of the fey, and as such were gifted with long life and supernatural senses and reflexes. It was with this speed and skill that they immediately drew their bows and fired a volley of precisely aimed arrows. The nearest dozen orcs were struck simultaneously, an arrow into each orc's breast as the elven metal pierced their boiled leather armor. To the shock and horror of the elves only two of them went down, the others rushing madly onwards despite their wounds.

The elves swallowed their surprise and fired a second volley, this time bringing three more to the ground. The last of the first wave neared the elves and raised their blades as another four of them went down with arrows riddling their bodies.

The elves reached into their quivers to draw forth fresh arrows as they looked into the faces of doom. Coming up the hill was the rest of the horde, all rushing wildly as if lost in a berserker rage. The elves knew that to run meant to be cut down from behind, so they stood their ground and fired point blank at the three who were closing in.

Ma-Gur bounded up the hill as the battle madness had carried him over so many miles burned brighter than ever at the long awaited sight of the enemy being slaughtered by the two surviving orcs who had reached the top. The young orc managed to catch an elf fumbling for another arrow as he crested the hill. The elf doubled over as he was thrown back by the power of the orc's blow, the gaping wound in his midsection spewing blood and entrails into the air as he fell. Ma-Gur did not stop running, instead he allowed his momentum to carry him into the next elf.

This one, however, was ready to receive the charge. The elf rushed under the large blade as Ma-Gur attempted to split her open with a power attack. The lithe warrior spun on the balls of her feet as she drew her thin blade across the passing orc's side. The wounded orc stumbled and fell to the ground kicking up dirt as the rolled to a stop.

The elf turned just in time to dodge another strike from a charging orc, ducking under the blade and driving the point of her sword through its diaphragm and into the heart. The orc's forward momentum was halted, its feet shooting out from under it as the elf slammed him to the ground by stepping forward. It was as if the orc were caught in a tide and she was the impassive cliff upon which he broke. The elf yanked her now blood blackened blade from her fallen foe and stood to face another.

Her eyes quickly scanned the battlefield, only to be disheartened by the sight of her comrades all lying in various stages of death and dying. The orcs weren't even finishing them off, so intent were they upon reaching the knights. Many orcs rushed by her, forcing her to duck and dive over and over as if she were in a stampede. Eventually a lucky blow disabled her sword arm as it knocked her to the ground. She had just managed to get back to her feet when an orc planted a spear in her belly as it ran by, not even bothering to collect it's weapon after she had fallen over dead.

Ma-Gur struggled to his feet, the wound in his side burning with a bittersweet pain. He was moving down the other side of the hill towards the circle of knights before he even realized what he was doing. The power came back to his body as he began to move again, the grip on his sword tightening in anticipation of battle. Ahead he could already see the first wave of orcs nearing the shocked knight's battle line. As he ran forward he witnessed the battle as it unfolded.

The first wave of orcs reached the knights just as the mounted warriors spurred their horses for a charge. The two forces met with the sounds of steel on steel and metal cleaving flesh. Under normal circumstances such a surprise charge tactic would have worked for the knights, a devastating attack that would drive the enemy back before them. Today it was not a successful action. Enhanced as they were by Ghalik's magic, the orcs were not easily knocked aside by the charging horses, nor were they harrowed by the flurry of blows rained upon them from the mounted warriors themselves. Naturally, some orcs were killed during the charge, but not nearly enough to make the tactic worth leaving the defenses of the circled wagons.

By the time Ma-Gur reached the fight it was well underway. The impending orc victory was already apparent from the swiftness in which the knights and their retainers seemed to be dying, but there was yet some killing to be done. He joined the fray with abandon, his sword swinging too and fro denting armor and carving flesh. Quickly, the fight turned against the knights, for though they had numerical superiority they had been outmaneuvered. The failed charge had forced the mounted warriors to fight in close quarters with the enemy while still on horseback. This gave the orcs on foot the option of slaying the horse, oftentimes pinning the knight under the weight of his fallen mount.

Soon the tide of battle reached the circle of wagons as the surviving knights fought a hasty retreat. The orcs pressed their advantage and continued to push forward, whittling down the numbers of their enemy as they went. Just as it appeared that the knights would be able to rally with the remaining retainers behind the makeshift wall of carts one of the wagons was sent into the air with the splintering sound of metal striking wood. Many eyes turned to old Ghalik as he bashed another cart into pieces with his now glowing eldritch waraxe.

A cheer went up amongst the orcs as they poured in through the freshly made gaps. They flowed over the stalwart knights and their retainers like an angry green tide. The noises of fighting died quickly as the last of the humans fell, a silent scream on his face as an orcish blade spilled his life out onto the ground. Still mad with lust for carnage the orcs began savagely dismantling the carts with their weapons and bare hands. With a sense of desperation they shattered wood, slaughtered the wounded, and some even turned to mutilating the dead. The Gor-Angir was not satisfied. Like madmen they twitched and spasmed, the fight still running hot in their blood.

It was then that Ghalik bellowed for their attention. They were so enthralled by the magical power in his voice that they could not help but to obey. The horde gathered around him at the center of the now demolished circle of wagons. The wizard's waraxe no longer glowed, but a palpable aura of power crackled around the bloated orc. He was still very much under the sway of the Gor-Angir, but he seemed to be able to maintain his composure with some effort.

Before him he held a young wounded knight by the hair. The human was on his knees at Ghalik's feet facing the crowd, upright only because the old wizard held him so. The Ghalik looked around him, his gaze meeting the now lighter red eyes of the assembled horde. For many long moments the orc warriors and the wizard stared at each other, none saying a word. The only sounds that could be heard were the cackling of the crows that had come to feed on the dead.

Slowly and deliberately Ghalik raised his axe, holding it aloft for all to see. Then, with surprising alacrity, brought it down upon the young knight's neck, severing the head. Ghalik threw the head at the feet of the horde, then spit his scorn upon the body. Having done that his knees buckled and he collapsed to the ground unconscious. The orcs stood in silence for a moment, then moved to plundering the dead, though all of them fell unconscious as well long before accomplishing their task. The Gor-Angir was a harsh ally, and had left them to their wounds and their exhaustion, alone.

Chapter 5

Ma-Gur slowly returned to awareness, the dull haze of his vision clearing. He still found it exceptionally difficult to move, the extreme physical rigors of the last several days had all taken effect. His bones creaked and his muscles ached as he rolled onto his back and sat up. He put his head in his hands and massaged his temples in an effort to sooth his now blinding headache. He stopped rubbing suddenly when he heard the sound of voices behind him. With determined effort he turned his body to face the sounds, the fact that it was after nightfall not affecting his keen orcish night vision.

Before him stood two short creatures with pale green skin and very long pointed ears. They were covered in tattoos and little bone trinkets, wickedly barbed spears held menacingly in their hands. *Goblins*, thought Ma-Gur. He should have known better than to fall asleep out in the open after a battle, especially in areas well known to be populated with the small warriors. At first Ma-Gur tensed for a fight as the two creatures approached him, spears leveled at him threateningly. But then the goblins pointed their spears away and moved towards him with open hands extended. Without even realizing what happening he instinctively took the hands he was offered and found himself helped to his feet.

Ma-Gur shook his head and looked about him, noticing that the clearing was full of goblins. Most of the other orcs had been helped to their feet and were being herded towards the center of the battlefield. He felt a gentle nudge on his thigh from one of the goblins and began to walk towards the apparent gathering point.

The young orc shouldered his way through the dazed mass of orcs until he reached the middle of the assembly. Before him, on a makeshift seat, was Ghalik. Next to the old wizard stood an armored goblin, and judging from the lack of metal armor in the present goblin ranks this suggested that it was

33

the leader. They appeared to be engaging in a very animated conversation. Though Ma-Gur could not comprehend the high-pitched chirping sounds that made up the goblin tongue, he did begin to get an idea of what had happened. The goblins must have come upon the battle site only shortly after the orcs had fallen. Because of something to do with Ghalik, the goblins had not looted and murdered the surviving orcs, instead they had helped. Odd indeed.

As Ma-Gur looked on Ghalik and the goblin chief finished their discussion. The armored goblin stepped back and the wizard made to address the assembled orcs.

"My comrades, a strange thing has happened this day. We have been sparred in our moment of weakness by those who would have normally murdered us without a thought or care. Their leader says that they have been following this army since yesterday. They kept their distance because of the elves, and when they became aware of our pursuit fled into the forest," Ghalik explained as he picked up his blood crusted waraxe and hung it upon it's place on his broad back. "They tell me that groups of these knights have been raiding all across the borders and now deeper in-country, displacing the goblin clans and even the troll tribes."

"He says that most efforts to combat them have failed because of their heavy cavalry and elvish allies, until now. The goblins want to join with us. They say that they can lead us to something they call the Meeting Stones. According to them it is the place where the other groups have made camp. I say we go to these Meeting Stones and get the others to join us as well. Then we can find a way to fight back, and drive those would-be heroes into the dirt," Ghalik spat as he emphasized his statement by stomping his foot heavily upon the blood-soaked soil.

Ghalik looked at the orcs expectantly, and one by one the orcs nodded their heads in acquiescence. Once the warriors had agreed to follow him, Ghalik turned to the armored goblin and extended his hand. The goblin leader filled Ghalik's hand with his own as he clapped the orc's meaty palm. At once a murmur of chirping went up among the goblins, who then began to fan out amidst the battlefield. The two groups made quick work of plundering the site, and soon the heavily armed group was ready to move out.

They went silently through the forest, the heavy orcs trying to match the almost feather-light step of the goblin clansmen. While a bargain had been struck by the leaders, tensions inevitably ran high as the group covered ground. It was obvious that not all of the goblins were supportive of their leader's decision to join up with the orcs instead of murdering them and looting their corpses. The orcs were able to pick up on those attitudes and reacted with an almost indignant hostility. However, everything was held in check by the two leaders who kept watchful eyes on their warriors and reproachful scowls on their faces.

The band of warriors carried on this way until well into the night, neither group willing to show weakness. Though eventually the longer stride of the orcs began to tell, and the goblins started to lag more and more behind. Seeing the situation as a potential breakup of the newly formed alliance, both Ghalik and the goblin chief agreed to call a halt for a time. Relieved, the exhausted warriors of both parties sank to the ground, too glad to be off their feet to remember to be hostile to each other.

Ma-Gur sat with his back to a tree and watched through tired eyes as Ghalik and the armored goblin talked. He wondered what the two creatures discussed, noticing that they often referred to a drawing or map of some sort they had drawn in the tough dirt. Personally he wasn't overly concerned with what the two discussed. He found that he trusted the old wizard to do what was best, be it a decision that meant his survival or death in battle. He was a warrior without a tribe. Just a warrior, whose one purpose was to fight and die. He was comfortable with that role. He was an orc, and one of the few remaining in the world who knew what that meant. What did these goblins think, he wondered. They had likely never seen such a display as they had witnessed earlier in the day. Perhaps it wasn't awe or the need for aid that had stayed their hands, perhaps it was fear.

The thought struck him like the blow of a hammer. That was it! They were afraid. He looked around at the goblin warriors, noticing for the first time that they were all men. Many of them were bearing well-concealed wounds, as if this force had seen battle not too many days before. A similar fate must have befallen the goblins as well as the Angir. The younglings and women slaughtered while the majority of the warriors were away. Now that he was paying attention he could almost detect the slight bitter scent of fear and defeat. It was a feeling that had been nagging at him all night. A palpable fear had crept insidiously into these lands.

Ma-Gur looked closer at the crude map that the two leaders were pouring over. He could just make out the sticks and stones that must have represented their combined forces. He could also see what appeared to be a battle line sweeping across the map in their direction. He grunted derisively as he turned his head and closed his eyes for sleep. Let them come.

The first rays of dawn filtered through the trees not long after, shining upon skin and armor until the heat and light awakened the sleeping warriors, they rose to their feet shaking the sleep from their bodies as they prepared to move on. Soon all were roused and standing, the order was given, and the day's journey began.

The orcs had regained much of their spent strength from their pursuit and battle with the knights. What vitality had been leeched away by the Gor-Angir seemed to be well on the way to being replenished. Though many of the orc's eyes had a reddish tint that never faded as long as they lived, a reminder of their past and likely future.

The day carried on much like the previous one, the orcs and goblins marching quietly along, putting mile after mile behind them. They rested at the end of the day, the orcs begrudgingly grateful for the begrudgingly generous goblins and their food rations. While orcs and goblins can out march any human alive, they suffer from hunger like all creatures. Once appetites were sated the group set watches and slept. So this routine was repeated for another day, the goblins and Okada foraging and hunting as the group pressed on. At the end of the third day of travel, just as the sun was setting on the horizon, they reached the Meeting Stones.

Chapter 6

A great many myths and legends surrounded the place of the Meeting Stones, most were lost in the haze of time and forgetfulness. Though there were some who remembered. Ca'tic'na was one who remembered. He was the goblin leader of the force that traveled with the orcs as well as the defacto authority over most other goblin clans on the north side of the Iithsulian border. While diminished in size, like all goblins, he was a formidable fighter and expert hunter. He was also one of the few loremasters left in this world; one of the few receptacles of knowledge about the old world that continued to slip into obscurity. Like Ghalik, he knew the true history of his race and that knowledge would die with he and his warriors. So it was with the ancient races of goblin and troll, even the immortal orcs, life was short so there was little time or use for history.

While Ghalik and his people lived high in the mountains surrounded by villages and fiefdoms yet away from the continent spanning empires of men, Ca'tic'na and his people lived right on the border between empires and wild lands. He had witnessed the vast numbers of fighting forces march out of Iithsul. He knew that the religious leaders of men had called for a crusade against the remnants of the old world. A genocidal holy war designed to carve out more of the world for what they called the good people.

He told Ghalik of these things, the old wizard never ceasing to amaze Ca'tic'na with his command of the goblin tongue. He told the orc about the lightning raid on his clanhome, a savage massacre resulting in the death of all, but he and the warriors who arrived too late to make any difference. The goblin chief was about to tell Ghalik about the dwarves when one of his scouts chirped a warning, they had arrived.

The place of the Meeting Stones was impressive indeed. A circular clearing in the thick woods nearly one hundred and fifty yards in diameter. Tall, ornately carved stone pillars ringed the clearing. Their tops curved inwards to give the illusion of claws coming out of the earth. Several campfires had been lit, shedding soft orange light into the coming night. Around these campfires sat an alarmingly large number of hulking, yellow skinned trolls. These creatures were taller than even the orcs. Their gangly muscular arms nearly as long as their entire bodies. They were clothed in threadbare loincloths and boiled leather armor and at their sides or in their hands the majority of them carried wickedly spiked cudgels or maces. One particularly large troll, undoubtedly the leader, stood to reveal a massive greatsword strapped across his back.

Ca'tic'na chirped a greeting as he entered the circle, the trolls relaxed and went back to their eating and talking. The troll leader approached Ca'tic'na, but suddenly stopped short with a threatening snarl when Ghalik and the orcs began stepping into the light. Immediately the trolls were on their feet and crowding behind their leader. The orcs reacted just as quickly, forming up to match the trolls as they bared their teeth and growled.

The goblins retreated in confusion, Ca'tic'na and his band joining the other clans forced to camp outside the circle of Meeting Stones. The goblin leader scowled guiltily, he had known this was going to happen. Yet he felt that in a goblin's life one must follow the strongest or none at all. After doing the bidding of the displaced trolls, he was glad to have found the orcs.

Ghalik immediately sensed the deception and finally understanding that Ca'tic'na's purpose in saving the orcs had been to use them to face up to the trolls. While he was angered with the conniving goblins, he understood their position. Perhaps Ca'tic'na's talks of fighting back were true, but the goblin's first priority had been to replace troll leadership with orcish authority. Ghalik smiled inwardly, Ca'tic'na was one of the few goblins that understood the almost mystical role of goblins as minions of stronger beings, at least the goblin chief knew why he was inclined to be subservient. That knowledge gave him the power to choose his masters, too bad that freedom would pass when his clan's time was ended.

The brutal intensity of the situation brought Ghalik's wandering mind back to his present surroundings. The two forces stood opposite each other, ready for the slightest indication from their leaders to attack. Sensing the hesitation, Ghalik stepped towards the troll leader, who moved to face him.

"I am Reygoth. I am master of this place. Who are you and why have you come here? Answer me quickly for my patience runs thin," commanded the troll as he planted the tip of his sword in the earth before him, his hands resting lightly upon the pommel.

Ma-Gur was outraged at such a blatant display of arrogance and disrespect for the Ghalik. With rage burning in his eyes, he took half a step forward, growling as he hefted his blade. Immediately his actions were mirrored by a troll standing near Reygoth, his mace ready for battle. The two squared off and were about to exchange the blows that would ignite a widespread blood bath when their respective leaders restrained them with harsh words. A mutual understanding seemed to pass between them as they once again resumed their conversation.

"It seems, troll, that you do not desire a fight any more than I do," mused Ghalik as the glimmer of an idea began to form in his mind.

"No, orc, we do not. Our numbers have been depleted by men, and it would shame us to die in the slaughtering of your people while there are still humans in the land," uttered Reygoth as he smiled savagely.

Again a tension seemed about to break as Ghalik took the subtle insult in stride. Only Reygoth noticed the tiny smile that briefly played across the Ghalik's face. It almost frightened him.

"We also have been set upon by men and their elven allies. It would be foolish to throw away warriors that could be used to fight the humans. Perhaps we should settle this the old way," the old wizard suggested.

"There is nothing to settle greenskin. Trolls rule here. You orcs should just move on," threatened Reygoth as he pointed away from the circle and into the darkness.

Ghalik's voice instantly grew deeper and more resonant. It was as if all audible sounds in the area ceased, leaving only the orcish wizard's voice booming in the air. The electric feeling in the area was the telltale sign that magic was afoot.

"Trial by combat," he uttered, the words so powerful it seemed that they would knock the troll over, "If a troll wins, we will leave. If an orc wins, we stay and we will lead."

Despite the magical potency of Ghalik's words Reygoth appeared unaffected, while behind him the assembled trolls all fell under the spell's influence, and began to nod their heads in agreement. Ghalik could see that Reygoth's willpower had managed to throw off the manacles of the spell, so reacted by making one last effort to control the situation.

"Ca'tic'na! To me!" he thundered, his spell enhanced voice booming through the woods.

For a long moment there wasn't a sound, then just as Reygoth was about to snort his disapproval, the goblins emerged from the wood. Not just Ca'tic'na's clan either, but all of the other clans as well. Diminutive in size, yet their numbers were staggering. As was the fact that they held their spears at the ready, and were moving up to flank the trolls.

Reygoth quickly realized that a fight would now be a guarantee defeat for the trolls. Perhaps they could beat the orcs, but not all of the greenskins at once. The glint of bloodlust had sparkled in the orcish wizard's eyes, almost daring the troll to order an attack. Reygoth could only see one way out, to do as Ghalik wished. Inwardly the spark of hope shone yet. Reygoth was a knowledgeable leader despite his quick temper, and he knew that possible subservience was better than assured annihilation.

"Fine, trial by combat," he muttered, taking a step back and placing his hand of the shoulder of the troll that almost came to blows with Ma-Gur, "Let the two so eager to draw blood decide this thing."

Ghalik nodded silently to Ma-Gur, who hefted his weapons and stepped forward. Ghalik whispered in his ear, "All great deeds are bathed in blood. Never forget."

A circle of orcs and trolls quickly formed around the two combatants. The occasional goblin had squeezed into witness the action, one of these was Ca'tic'na. His eyes went wide as he looked into the circle. Right in front of him stood two warriors entering into ritual combat. *How odd*, he thought, *that these orcs and trolls were using the place of Meeting Stones for such things.* Only Ca'tic'na remembered the stories and legends. Only he knew the tales of the sacrifices made by vast armies here. Who before battle would hold ritual combats to consecrate their war efforts with spilt blood. It was held that victory was assured when the stones shook as a sign of the god's approval. He had no idea what that would mean, but still he stood enthralled as history unknowingly repeated itself.

Ma-Gur and the troll looked across the makeshift arena at each other. The menace and hostility was electrifying and contagious. Threatening snarls and growls filled the circle as Ghalik and Reygoth held their forces in check. The two leaders exchanged glances, then simultaneously nodded and held their right hands in the air. The silent pause was deafening, all that could be heard was breathing and the creak of armor as everyone waited for the fight to begin. Without warning the two leaders chopped the air with their hands as they lowered them, signaling the beginning of the match.

Ma-Gur and the troll roared their battle cries and charged straight towards each other. The troll ran forward madly, raising his giant mace to the sky.

Ma-Gur had slung his shield onto his back and charged the troll with his cleaving sword held in both hands. It seemed like an eternity before the combatants finally collided.

The massive troll brought his club down at the same instant Ma-Gur swung his sword. The two weapons met in midair with a grating clash as sparks flew from the great impact. Their strikes mutually thwarted, their parry became a test of strength as both troll and orc locked their weapons and began to push.

Ma-Gur was the largest orc in the tribe other than old Ghalik and had quickly become known in the tribe for his size and strength. Always being the strongest, and never having fought a troll, led Ma-Gur to make the mistake of entering a contest of strength with his opponent. For a few moments the two warriors seemed evenly matched, but as muscles creaked and the tension built the troll's superiority began to show. Ma-Gur was slowly forced downwards by the impossibly strong troll. Soon Ma-Gur was on one knee, barely staying on his feet under the combined weight and strength of the troll warrior.

The deadlock was broken when the troll lashed out with his foot in a vicious kick to Ma-Gur's ribs. The force of the blow picked the orc up off the ground and sent him sailing through the air until he finally skidded to a halt. Covered in dirt and grime, Ma-Gur quickly forced himself to his feet. He grabbed his aching side and spit a gob of blood onto the ground, the pain of his old wound mingling with the new. He turned as he heard the troll snarl and close in for the kill.

Without his sword he was defenseless; it lay far from him and the troll was now between he and it. Remembering his shield, the orc slipped in onto his forearm and braced for the assault. It came as the troll closed in on the young orc swinging its mace as it advanced. Ma-Gur managed to duck the first swipe, then side step the second. The third however, hit him with a glancing blow to the thigh, knocking him to the ground.

The troll tried to splatter him as the lay on the ground, but he managed to roll out of the way just in time. While the troll's guard was down, Ma-Gur hurled his shield at the troll's face, the edged metal breaking its nose. While the troll reeled from the pain, Ma-Gur made a desperate run for his sword, hoping his luck held as he heard the troll's enraged pursuit from behind him.

The young orc pumped his legs with all his might, building up speed as he dashed for the fallen sword. He could see it lying in the dirt before him, he was almost there. Just as he neared it he felt and heard the troll bearing down on him. With a desperate yell Ma-Gur dove for the blade, but at that instant his injured leg gave out underneath him. The orc hit the dirt face first and his hand plowing a gouge through the loamy earth as he still single-mindedly went for his sword.

The troll let out a cry of victory as he raised his mace to deliver the blow that must surely finish this ornery opponent. Ma-Gur's bruised fingers found the handle of his weapon and closed around it. As the troll brought the mace down towards the fallen orc, Ma-Gur rolled over onto his back bringing his sword around to parry the blow. The head of the mace buried itself in the soft ground as it missed its intended target. The troll lost his balance and stumbled forward, almost falling completely over. Before the troll could recover Ma-Gur, still on the ground, launched himself upward to deliver a bone crushing left hook punch to the unbalanced troll's jaw.

The sound of the troll's jaw breaking echoed through the night as he stumbled a few steps away from the young orc. This gave Ma-Gur the chance to back away and bring his sword up into a guard position. The troll had managed to regain his balance and get his mace back into both hands. For a moment the two opponents looked silently at each other, then as Ma-Gur saw the half-conscious look in the still punch-drunk troll's eyes, he attacked.

The orc warrior advanced on the dazed troll, who managed to snap out of his stupor just in time to block the first sword slash. Quickly realizing that he was faster than the now near blind troll, Ma-Gur pressed his attack hurling strike after strike at the larger warrior. The troll was a skilled fighter, but was wounded and slow. With his heavy mace he wasn't able to effectively parry the lighter and faster sword assaults. It was not long until the orc's blade had hacked a large chunk out of the troll's leg, quickly followed by a deep gash in the troll's head from a glancing blow.

Enraged and injured, the troll leveled one last swing at the orc warrior. A blow so powerful that the earth shook as Ma-Gur leapt out of the way, causing the mace to bury itself in the earth once more. Seizing the opportunity, Ma-Gur brought his sword down onto the troll's outstretched arms. The troll fell back onto the ground as both of its arms were severed midway up the forearm. Ma-Gur finished it off by driving the point of his weapon through the troll's heart and into the ground below.

The crowd was silent, knowing better than to cheer or boo at such crucial moments. Reygoth and Ghalik walked out into the circle, each standing next to his chosen warrior.

"It seems that we trolls are fated to follow you greenskin," stated Reygoth with an uncommon air of respect, something it seemed quite difficult for him to allow to surface, "Your warrior represents you well. It seems then that you are welcome to this camp. Who are you?"

"Ghalik. In my language that word is both name and title. As to my warriors, they are the Gor-Angir," the wizard informed him calmly.

"What is it that you seek?" Reygoth asked as Ghalik turned and gestured for his warrior to move forward and make camp.

"In short, vengeance. But this talk can wait. First let us cool the warfires between our people. We make peace with each other, then we will decide upon who to make war first," Ghalik answered as he and Reygoth walked towards the center of camp, where a makeshift throne had been erected. Undoubtedly for Reygoth, but now the orcs were throwing down groundcloth and supplies at its base. There was no mistake who was in charge now.

"Let us find that cunning little goblin Ca'tic'na. Then we will hold a war council. The three of us have to find how best to sell our lives in the annihilation of our enemies," the old wizard uttered as he ascended his new throne.

Chapter 7

"Ma-Gur, awaken," called a voice through the blissful haze of well-earned sleep. The sleeping orc would normally have ignored it, yet the urgency in the voice stirred him. The young orc opened his eyes to find Okada standing near him, his eyes still faintly glowing red from their contact with the killing spirit.

"What is it?" muttered the rising warrior as he strapped on his boots and collected his weapons. His leg and side still pained him greatly, but he refused to show the on looking ranger as he stood to join him.

"Ghalik. He is in council with the goblin and troll leaders. He says that each leader is bringing two of their own warriors. It seems we have earned his attentions," stated Okada as the two orcs hurried towards Ghalik's throne area.

Ma-Gur silently walked alongside the smaller orc. Why had he been chosen? Of all the other better, more experienced warriors, why him? Okada was an obvious choice, he was the best hunter and pathfinder the tribe had produced for centuries. Why a young and relatively unproven fighter?

As if seeing the questioning look on the younger orc's face, Okada answered, "He sees something in you. That's why you were chosen."

Okada immediately came to a halt, pointing his long finger at Ma-Gur's broad chest.

"But don't you think he means to further your glory. Ghalik is what is best, and worst, in all of us. So yes, be proud of his attention, it speaks highly of you. But always remember that he is using you for his own purpose. Even though his is the greatest of all our leaders, he is still an orc, and so are you," Okada rasped.

Then, calmly as if nothing had been said, Okada turned and continued walking. Leaving Ma-Gur standing alone in confusion, "Come on little brother, we don't want to keep him waiting," the pathfinder chuckled as Ma-Gur hurried to catch up.

They walked in silence the rest of the way. Shortly they emerged into the throne area, now the hoard point for all of the extraneous possessions of the three groups. At first the trolls were unhappy about the command to give up their extra belongings, but soon were shown the wisdom and gain in everyone sharing commonly. Now everyone was well fed and armed. Goblin hunting and foraging parties returned often, loaded down with game and roughage. While troll and orc construction crews cut down trees and hewed them into useable logs which were piled up for some as yet undisclosed purpose.

Ghalik's wisdom and authority had turned a refugee camp into a military outpost, and the morale of all three groups had increased significantly. All three races seemed united towards a common goal and everyone felt as if great things were on the horizon.

At the center of it all stood Ghalik, next to his newly claimed throne, dressed in wolf skins against the cold. By his side stood Reygoth and Ca'tic'na, each accompanied by two warriors from their own tribes. As Okada and Ma-Gur approached Ghalik nodded and gestured for them to take their places amongst the ranks of the other warriors. Everything was arranged to both physically and symbolically represent the hierarchy of the camp. On the throne sat Ghalik, below him on the supporting raised dias stood Reygoth and Ca'tic'na, and below them on the ground stood the six warriors.

"Now that we are all here, I would like to begin," Ghalik stated as he waved a hand for all to be seated. Reygoth and Ca'tic'na had small unassuming chairs of their own, the warriors were forced to sit on the ground.

His voice rising above the tumult of the bustling camp, Ghalik spoke, "We have joined our forces. What once were now three groups of displaced people are now an army. Our numbers may pale against the might of these allied armies that harry us, but the trolls are strong and the goblins cunning. We orcs are the bridge between, we have strength and cunning enough to fight on both fields. The glue that holds us together is the enemy. Their attacks have made this alliance, so let them choke on it."

"Now we have an outpost, a sanctuary from which to strike. Which brings me to Ca'tic'na and his goblins," rasped the old wizard.

Upon hearing his name, the goblin leader stood and turned to face Ghalik. Of those non-goblins assembled the orcish wizard was the only one able to understand the little man. The goblin began speaking, his chirping voice full of excitement as he spoke with Ghalik. The old wizard relayed the goblin's words to the rest of the group, translating Ca'tic'na's rapid speech as quickly as he could.

"Ca'tic'na says that in their time on the borders south of here the goblins discovered that the human and elf forces have been receiving aid from a nearby dwarven fortress, Ameran."

The revelation caused an outraged rumble deep in the throats of some of the warriors. It was well known that the dwarves kept to themselves, preferring to quarry their stone and smelt their precious metals than to get mixed up in the affairs of the outside world. Their involvement now was testament to their greed or intolerance for the ancient races, either of which condemned then in the eyes of all gathered around the throne that night.

"He says that they have been supplying the crusaders with weapons and supplies, as well as free passage through their lands. It will not be long before they begin adding detachments of troops to the crusader armies," Ghalik translated.

"What are we going to do about it? Everyone knows that when battle comes the stone men go to ground. How are we supposed to fight them, invade their stronghold?" snorted Reygoth as he folded his arms across his chest disapprovingly, his ego still bruised from the loss of his throne.

"Yes," Ghalik uttered as he looked hard at the group, his confidence and determination radiating about him.

Reygoth was still unconvinced.

"How?"

"My ranger Okada is going to go with a goblin hunting party into the dwarven lands. Their mission will be two fold. First they are going to pick out a few good raiding opportunities like villages or supply lines. While word is sent back to inform us they will continue on towards the stronghold. Hopefully they will be able to locate a weakness that we can exploit," explained Ghalik as he smiled toothedly, "Then we attack."

"But do we have sufficient siege equipment?" Reygoth questioned, still reluctant to go along with Ghalik's seemingly mad scheme.

"Every stronghold has a weakness, just like every suit of armor. Once we find that weakness, there will be no siege. We will see just how far too ground the stone men can go when we begin raiding their lands. Perhaps we will be able to draw them out and then take the citadel while the majority of their warriors are away. If we bide our time whilst our scouts bring us information, we can win," Ghalik responded, his enthusiasm for the plan showing in his gleaming eyes.

Reygoth said no more, apparently satisfied for the moment with Ghalik's answer.

"You warriors were assembled to listen to this war council. Go now and tell all of what you have heard. If all of us know our mission then all will proceed as planned," commanded the Ghalik as he descended from his throne. "Okada take your rest while you can. The goblin's will wake you when all is prepared. Now go."

Okada did as he was bidden giving Ma-Gur a knowing look and disappearing into the camp. Ma-Gur stood and walked purposefully into the orc encampment. As he neared the fires of his comrades he could see that word of his involvement had spread quickly and everyone was waiting for news. Remembering Ghalik's orders he raised his hands in greeting, then began his retelling of the meeting and informing the Gor-Angir of the old wizard's scheme.

No questions were asked of Ma-Gur when he was finished speaking. All present had heard him clearly in the nighttime silence. The plan was simple, yet it hinged dearly upon the success of Okada and the goblin scouts, so an anxious energy crept into the encampment.

As the night wore on, many warriors, and not just orcs, could not sleep. Their thoughts were with the orc ranger and his goblin raiders who stole away in the dead of night. There were ten goblins all told, silently gripping their spears as they stealthily blended into the night. Okada was not the woodsman that the goblins were, yet was as accomplished as any orc possibly could be in the stealthy arts. He too crept out of his shelter, shouldered his stolen elvish bow, and followed the fast paced goblins into the night.

For nearly five days life at the outpost went on as it had on the day before the hunting party's departure. Food was secured, wood was gathered and weapons were cared for. Ghalik had revealed his purpose in having so much wood and food stored; he intended for the army to live on their nourishment and warmth once the dwarven stronghold was taken. His rationale being that the dwarves would likely poison their supplies before the invaders could stop them. The old wizard had also conscripted a large number of the more nimble fingered goblins to begin making coils of rope. The more coils, he insisted, the less time that will be lost moving the army should rope be required.

The barely suppressed anxiety was worked out as everyone went about their tasks, until near dusk on the sixth day. A cry went up from the sentries as one of the goblin scouts from Okada's party came running into the camp.

By the time the goblin reached Ghalik's throne the entire camp had dropped what they were doing and hurried to listen. As they gathered round they could see the goblin making his report in the chirping language of goblin kind. Total silence fell as Ghalik stood to face the crowd.

"They have found all that we had hoped for and more! The land is ripe for our vengeance!" bellowed Ghalik. The crowd descended into roars of excitement, but were quickly silenced by Ghalik's booming voice.

"But the enemy is upon us! Another force of crusaders comes at us from the east. We must pack and move quickly, lest our fire be quenched before it is given the chance to brighten!"

The six elven rangers skirted the circle, staying to the tree line as they made their way. Carefully they emerged from the forest and into the ring of ancient stones, their arrows knocked and bows at the ready. Keen eyes took in the scene before them as their breath came out, cloudlike in the morning chill.

The camp had been abandoned, and hastily at that. All about the area were the deep ruts from sleds or wagons, gouges left in the earth by heavy vehicles. Tracks of troll, goblins, and orc could all be seen. The path they had taken was fairly obvious, the underbrush around what seemed to have originally been a game trail hacked and churned as the horde passed through it.

The elves gathered together in the center of the stone circle, signaling to the other six elves waiting in the trees, sending them back to the main body of troops with a report of what had been seen. The rest of them began talking in hushed tones, discussing the terrifying implications of the abandoned camp. Apparently troll, orc, and goblin had formed an alliance of some kind. Aside from the fact that most of the goblin tracks were in the back of the fleeing column it appeared that it was a bloodless alliance. The elves wondered at the danger such cooperation amongst the ancient races would pose to the world if it spread to other enclaves of these creatures. They would be facing thousands of insurmountable foes for sure. Hearing the Iithsulian force drawing near, four of the elves stayed behind to relay the new plan. While the other two moved up the new trail to pursue the fleeing horde.

Chapter 8

The goblins were running hard without a care for stealth or silence as they plowed through the underbrush at incredible speeds. Their wilderness skills giving them an added advantage along with their short stature. They were able to follow obscure game trails with speed and not be impeded by hanging foliage that would have stalled taller creatures. There were only a handful of them left now, though they had begun the day with many more.

The outset of the day had seen them scampering about the forest laying a myriad of traps and snares along the fleeing horde's main trail as well as the smaller side trails the elves were sure to take. Their small force had been chosen by the big orc leader to be a rearguard. Though all who knew of the order understood that rearguard meant ambush party, at least that was what the word meant in goblin. So after several hundred yards of trail had been trapped the goblins hastily concealed themselves at the entrance to the trapped area. Some perching in trees, others squatting in makeshift blinds and others still were hidden amongst the underbrush.

They knew that the force they were about to attack not only outnumbered them, but had an advance scout troupe of elves. Elves and goblins have long been dire enemies, each representing the more primitive and wild natures of sentient beings. Yet the goblins were an ancient race bound to the earthen roots of the past so deeply that it was whispered by more radical thinkers that the goblins were likely not just an ancient race, but the First Race. The elves, always a prideful and aloof race, were threatened by this assertion in ways that only such elegant and powerful creatures could be. The very idea of the short greenskins being the rightful keepers of the forest ruined the stoic composure of the graceful race. It was a blood feud that had lasted for centuries. The majority of the world's wild places held by the elves who professed harmony with nature, and the northern lands occupied by goblins who simply were the land. Even then they had to share the north with ever increasing numbers of human settlers, orcs, and even dwarves. Only against elven enemies did goblin warriors do battle without fear or the coercion of leadership.

And so it was that the goblin bushwhackers waited patiently in their hiding places, their pulses racing as the smell of elf registered from downwind. Soon the smell was accompanied by sounds, far to slight for humans or even orcs to detect, but loud enough to be heard by the keen ears of the goblins. As they waited silently, eight elves came into view, spread out across the wood so that no single ambusher could take them all at once. They walked with bows at the ready, their eyes scanning the forest for signs of any threat.

It was unclear if the elves noticed the goblins before or after the attack, for almost simultaneously the elves gasped and began to launch arrows into the forest while the goblins surged from their hiding places and hurled spears at their foes. The bushwhackers began to go down clutching arrows to their breasts as the elves rapid fired their sleek projectiles. The battle was short-lived however, as a shower of barbed spears rained down upon the elves from every direction. Within moments all of the elves lay dead, unable to dodge the multitude of thrown weapons.

Yet the battle was not quite over because four more elves materialized out of the woods firing arrows with deadly accuracy as they came. There was a brief exchange of fire when the goblins recovered from the counterattack and hurled their remaining spears. Two of the elves went down. Their lithe bodies contorted in pain as the goblin spears pierced their flesh. The remaining elves stood resolute as they dropped their bows and drew their long knives while the goblins closed in, their wickedly curved shortswords held aloft.

As the goblins rushed the elves, a great commotion sounded. The bushwhackers were too busy fighting to notice that the knights and their footmen had now caught up to the elves. The two elves fought valiantly, claiming several lives as they danced from opponent to opponent, but were both laid low by the sheer number of goblins they faced. Before the green skinned rangers could celebrate their victory however, the humans were upon them.

Shouting battle cries and waving their weapons the men of Iithsul charged. The goblins, knowing they were outmatched, scattered and attempted to flee into the safety of the woods. Some were killed in the charge, but most of the survivors made it into cover. The situation soon became a running battle as the human warriors fanned out and gave chase. They were able to move quickly because of their long stride, but the goblins were able to move faster in the tangled underbrush. The main body of surviving goblins eventually outpaced the humans and escaped into the forest. What stragglers there were soon fell to the blades of their determined pursuers. The human pursuit from that point on was significantly slowed as they began to fall dead to the traps and snares placed by the goblins to cover their escape.

The goblins had been running since then. Now the sun was beginning to set, and they were exhausted. They knew that the humans would not be far behind, so they must warn the army of the pursuing foe. The goblins crossed a stream running red with what could only have been blood, avoiding the burned bridge as they opted to ford the shallow waters. They crested the hill to find that they gazed down into a small village.

As they carefully approached they could see the horde's camp at the top of the hill across the valley. Form the wisps of smoke rising from the town and the smell of burnt flesh, it took little imagination for the goblins to deduce what had happened. Expert trackers that they were, it took only a small effort to see the story of the raid in the kicked up dirt and the corpses of the fallen. Like most settlements in these parts, this village was no doubt one of the supply towns for the dwarven stronghold. Growing crops and raising livestock for the dwarven larders in exchange for protections and well-crafted dwarven metals. There were no walls or gates to the town, it must have been a slaughter.

The goblins felt no pity as they moved through the village, which had been picked clean of plunder. No doubt several of the warriors in the horde would be sporting dwarven weapons and armor. While they were disappointed not to have had a chance at spoils, they did get to kill some elves and most goblins were simple folk with simple pleasures.

The goblins could see that Ghalik had put all of the harvested wood to use in their absence. Now that the army possessed all of the wagons, carts, and mules of the burned village below, there was no need for the sleds. So the wood had been split into planks and lashed together with rope, which consequently they noticed a group of goblins still weaving even more coils of. These lashed planks were currently being used as makeshift walls in various parts of the camp, placed so that they would impede an advancing foe but not cut off the horde's escape.

A call went up form the sentries as the bushwhackers returned. They were quickly ushered to Ghalik's now portable throne. He sat in silence, with Reygoth and Ca'tic'na on either side of him, as he listened to their chirping report. Upon hearing of their pursuit he frowned, but beyond that did not seem worried. When they were done he thanked them, gave them permission to select spoils from the leftovers in the community wagon and had food brought to them. He then gestured for Reygoth and Ca'tic'na to accompany him as he walked into the night.

"So are we going to fight them?" asked Reygoth as he walked alongside the old wizard.

"I have yet to decide that. On the one hand we could carry on as we have, raid the next village and wait for Okada's return. But if we do that this new threat will surely put us between themselves and the dwarves," Ghalik grumbled as he looked out over the burned village.

"Perhaps we could do both," Reygoth suggested, "We could leave a small force of trolls and orcs here to ambush the humans while we take the rest of the horde and press on."

Ghalik thought to himself for a moment, turning the idea over and over in his mind. He discussed it with Ca'tic'na in a rapid exchange of the goblin tongue. After a few moments of silence following the exchange, Ghalik stopped walking. The look of his face betrayed the fact that his decision had been made.

"We will leave a detachment of orcs and trolls here while the rest of us move on. They will hide themselves in the remnants of the village. Should our enemies enter the town, our forces will do battle there. If they skirt the village to hasten their pursuit, our warriors will have them in a vice, and sooner or later we will turn and fight as they are cut down from behind," he explained as he once again began walking, this time back towards the camp, "Reygoth, select a third of your warriors and have them assembled at my throne as soon as is possible. We will lay the trap tonight, just in case they have advance scouts who can see our fires."

Within the hour Ma-Gur found himself at the head of a force that was nearly a third of the entire horde. At first Reygoth chaffed at the idea of the trollslayer being in command, but a few wise words from Ghalik about Ma-Gur's popularity with the orcs and prowess against the late troll champion would do well to ensure that he was obeyed. And so it was that the strike force carefully bedded down in the ruins of the village.

The rest of the army was up and moving just before dawn, packing up supplies and heading off into the hills to pursuer their raiding campaign against the dwarves and their allies. The strike force awakened to the commotion of the moving horde, then strained their ears against the silence left in its wake. For long hours they waited, orc and troll, impatient for the fighting to begin but disciplined enough to stay in cover.

It was just around noon, when the sun was at its zenith, that the sounds of hoof beats and marching could be heard. The hidden warriors tensed as they heard the sounds come near. *It was working*, thought Ma-Gur as he listened to the humans enter the village. Only moments now until they were far enough into town that they could be bushwhacked. Armored horses moved into Ma-Gur's field of vision, close enough to touch. He quickly and silently emerged from the broken doorway he had been hidden behind and attacked.

The knight never saw it coming. The orc's heavy blade cleaving through his leg and into the horse's flank. As his legs separated from his body he toppled off his dying horse, only to be pinned by its dead weight as it landed on top of him. The knight next in the column was just able to deflect Ma-Gur's blow with his shield, but was soundly unhorsed by the powerful swing of an ambushing troll's stout club. The knight landed in a heap as the survivors of the initial attack struggled on.

Ma-Gur felt as if there was something the matter, in spire of the one-sided battle raging around him. Using the powerful muscles in his arms, he lifted himself onto the only partially destroyed roof of the building he had been hiding in. As he gained a purchase and steadied himself he looked out across the town and the hills from whence the enemy had come. Ma-Gur was surprised and shaken by what he saw there.

Only about a third of the enemy forces had moved into the village. The majority of the knights had remained in the open alongside their supply wagons while the footmen escorted the scant few knights that had moved in to investigate the village. Ma-Gur cursed as he realized that they hadn't been completely fooled, but true to his nature, put them out of his mind and leapt once again into the battle below.

The battle was swift and brutal, the human numbers had been reduced heavily during the initial assault. Yet they fought with the determination and tenacity that came with the knowledge and understanding of victory or death. Casualties on both sides were mounting, but in the close quarters fighting that was so common in cities, the pure brutality of the orcs and trolls was telling. Soon it was over, the humans killed to a man.

Ma-Gur was quick to reassemble his troop around the town square, knowing that he must act quickly.

"The humans must know by now that we are a threat, but they do not know how few we are compared to them. We cannot engage them in the field or their cavalry will run us down. But if we spread out over the village, perhaps we can fool them into thinking that our entire army resides here," he spoke as he pointed in the direction of the Iithsulian force.

"What would that accomplish?" bickered a gangly-armed troll, "Other than show the humans that we would rather hide than fight."

His statement was echoed by many of the troll warriors, even some of the orcs, who were obviously wondering the same thing.

"If they think the whole army is here, then they will concentrate on fighting us, and not pursuing our brothers," Ma-Gur answered, the red in his eyes bristling at the implied challenge.

The young orc stood defiant as he gazed menacingly at the assembled warriors, silently daring them to debate. He had managed to maneuver them into a position that would make any who did not go with his plan seem like fools for wanting to fight in the open or cowards if they fled. This realization sunk in as the thunderous sounds of hooves signaled a movement in the enemy ranks. Ignoring the sound Ma-Gur held his eyes fixed upon the crowd, entering into an unspoken test of wills with those less inclined to follow his lead. For a moment all that could be heard was the sound of the moving forces outside the town. Then one troll who stood at the back of the gathering spoke.

"Enough of this! Reygoth and the greenskin wizard chose him to lead us. They would not have done that without good reason. I say his wisdom is sound!" shouted the troll as he shouldered his mace and walked towards the sound of the enemy's position.

"Maybe we were left behind to die," argued the first dissenting troll.

"Does it matter? It is likely that we were, but we can sell our lives at a high cost," Ma-Gur retorted as he too moved to walk towards the enemy, "I, for one, would rather die with a spear in my chest than in my back. I know you want to fight and fight you shall, but here, on our terms, not theirs."

With that the group dispersed, even the disgruntled troll, who shrugged at the suicidal logic of the orcs as he hefted his club and followed. He preferred a stand up and fight compared to all of these underhanded war tricks, though he had to admit that they were outmatched and outnumbered. Maybe this was the best way to win.

Chapter 9

The orc and troll warriors dispersed among the ruins of the village. Some allowed themselves to be seen standing in the streets and alleyways facing the approaching enemy, while others took to the rooftops and balconies of the ruined buildings. Though they were fewer in number than the oncoming enemy the defenders had spread themselves along the edges of town in such a way that from the outside looking in it appeared that a much larger force waited in the village's winding streets.

At first it seemed as if the humans were going to bypass the ruined settlement, cutting their losses and continuing the pursuit. Yet as their outriders neared the village and saw its defenders, the column of knights turned towards town. While a full third of their forces had been wiped out, the humans still made deadly and numerous foes. Armored knights upon muscled warhorses led the way while the remaining companies of men at arms followed behind. A small handful of footmen stayed with the supply wagons as the primary force marched forward.

Upon seeing that the knights had taken the bait, the orcs and trolls pulled back deeper into the village. The knights became grim and set their jaws, this would be a nasty fight uprooting the evil house by house. The orcs and trolls knew it as well. This would be a battle lost and won street by street, blood spilt on both sides would mark every gain or loss of even an inch of ground.

Not wishing to meet a similar fate as their comrades, the approaching knights dismounted when they neared the village. The advantage of being mounted would not hold here in the narrow streets. The warriors had to be free to move and fight in such close quarters. The humans marched into the town shoulder to shoulder as they prepared for battle.

Not assault met them when they reached the outskirts of the village, so they spread out and moved cautiously down the alleyways and streets in groups of two and three. Men at arms rushed into nearby buildings, searching for hidden ambushers. For long moments the only sounds that could be heard were those of the humans pushing their way deep into the heart of the village.

Then, without warning, and inhuman cry went up from the village as orc and troll warriors emerged for battle. Many came rushing down the open streets to clash with the humans head on, while others lashed out from ruined buildings as yet unchecked by the men at arms. Shaken yet not undaunted by the onslaught of the enemy, the humans stood their ground as battle was joined.

The main body of the orc and troll force had rushed into open combat without much care for strategy or cunning. Ma-Gur couldn't blame them. They were not soldiers who followed orders, but individual warriors who had to follow their own instincts. It was all he could do to attempt to guide them, hoping to make at least their timing uniform. They had decided that when the humans reached the old foundry building they would attack. It was a large building that all could see from whatever their vantage point was. Beyond that simple matter of timing the orcs and trolls fought however they pleased.

Ma-Gur paid little mind to this fact, nor took offense or felt his leadership questioned. He knew just as well as everyone else did the way that such warriors were. The young orc himself was one of them. According to the stories and lessons he learned as a child around the campfires of his people, orcs had little use for strategy instead preferring to merely ride the current of battle to its natural conclusion. It was said by many, even begrudgingly by their enemies, that of all the races of the world it was the orcs who had the superior talent for tactics. Empathy for the ebb and flow of battle and the adaptability to use that as an advantage without fear or hesitation.

It was this mastery that gave Ma-Gur the confidence that allowed him to banish the worry and doubt of his force's ability to win. Even if eventual defeat was the inevitable result for bloodthirsty immortals, they would walk to their deaths over the corpses of their enemies.

These contemplative thoughts passed through Ma-Gur's mind as quickly as they came, replaced by the maddening din of battle as Ma-Gur joined the fight. He burst forth from a building near the middle of the now roiling struggle. As the orc cut down the soldier nearest him, he found that from the doorstep he could see much of the battle carrying on around him. The trolls, cliquish as ever, had grouped together and were mowing through the ranks of humans. Their massive bludgeons crushing bone and armor, laying low scores of humans in the tight press of bodies in the narrow streets.

The orcs seemed to have ended up in two groups. One had stayed relatively uniform in its formation, a tough wedge of green skin and steel that fought toe to toe with the stalwart knights. The second group was enmeshed with the majority of the men at arms, not pushing their line back, but holding them in place as the trolls came at them from the other side.

A few orcs had followed Ma-Gur's example, and had waited inside buildings and on rooftops for opportunities at ambushing the foe. These ambushers soon found themselves battling the stragglers that were not involved in the thick of the fighting.

Ma-Gur took in all of this with a moment's glance, then returned to his own task. Behind him in the building from which he had come were a handful of orcs and the troll who had spoken in his defense, Orvo. The small band followed Ma-Gur as he hacked and hewed his way through the loose formation of the men at arms already fighting other orcs. Ma-Gur did not focus upon killing his opponents, but merely passing through them. Using his shield as a weapon he bashed down those who stood in his way, lashing out with his blade if the opportunity presented itself. So it was with the rest of his small band as they followed in his wake, dispatching those who drew to near.

The band reached the other side of the battle, having only lost a few warriors in the process. Their goal was not the battle in the village, but the supply wagons waiting in the fields beyond. Ma-Gur left the village at a dead run, followed by the orcs and quickly outpaced by the long-legged Orvo. The few guards that remained soon forgot the welfare of their comrades and piled into the wagons, whipping the horses into action. At such a distance the wagons stood a chance of being able to escape the pursuing enemy.

There were six wagons in all. Each laden with food and supplies, making them move slower than the guards had hoped. Soon Orvo's long legs carried him within striking distance, and with one massive blow sent both driver and guard flying off the front seat in a jumble of blood and limbs. One of the guards in the back of the wagon managed to drive his spear deep into Orvo's shoulder, though the troll did not seem to notice as he bolted towards the next wagon.

The last two wagons in line, both having lost their drivers and Orvo rushed after the third, a second spear in his side, slowed their pace almost to a crawl. The remaining guards inside the wagons attempted to retake the reigns and move on, but by then the orcs were upon them. Ma-Gur vaulted over the rear of the wagon, both hands steadying himself as he slammed both of his feet into a guard's chest. As that guard was flung from the wagon by the blow the last one set upon Ma-Gur with his pointed shortsword. Not bothering to parry Ma-Gur sidestepped the blade and drove his shoulder into the chest of the oncoming guard. The human fell to the floor of the cart, he began to rise again but his ascent was cut short by Ma-Gur's heavy blade.

The orc looked up from his victim to witness Orvo charge the first wagon in the line. The rest of the supply carts had slowed and were being overrun by the orcs. The two guards in the back of the remaining cart were following the example set by their fallen comrades and hurling spears at the pursuing troll. Orvo, whose body was already wounded by spear and blade, finally fell as the two spears thrown from the cart buried themselves in his chest. The troll went to the ground without a sound, his life seeping away as the moments went on. The lone cart escaped into the woods.

The orcs came to a halt near Orvo's body, all panting heavily from their excruciating pursuit. There was no catching the escaped cart, so without much more than a callous glance at the valiant troll's corpse, the raiders returned to the captured wagons. Eager to discover what lay in the sacks and crates that burdened each one.

As the orcs brought the carts around and grouped them together, Ma-Gur stood on the seat of his wagon and looked back towards the village. The sounds of fighting could still be heard, but not nearly so much as when the battle had begun. It sounded as if a victor had been established, what could be heard was the mopping up phase of the fight. The orc gestured for two of his remaining warriors to follow him, and he made his way back towards the village, leaving the others to guard the newly acquired supplies.

They ran at a steady pace, conserving their energy should they need to rejoin the battle. Soon they reached the outskirts of town, the sounds of battle had become more sporadic, slowly dying out as the orcs drew ever nearer. The orcs gripped their weapons tightly and advanced into the ruined town.

Suddenly, as if they had appeared from thin air, a cluster of five human men at arms came careening towards the three orcs. Reacting as all good warriors would, the orcs immediately responded to what they perceived as an attack. The two orc warriors squared off with the oncoming humans as Ma-Gur moved up to meet the charge. He deflected a clumsy sword thrust with his shield and brought his blade down upon the swordsman. The heavy weapon connected with the human's collarbone and cleaved through to his heart. As the first human fell the other soldiers faltered, losing the momentum of their rush. They fell easy prey to orc blades as the three greenskinned warriors pressed their advantage. When the flurry of blows had ceased all of the men at arms had fallen, and one of the orcs had lost a hand.

The three warriors continued deeper into the village as the wounded orc field dressed his wound. They could no longer hear the sounds of battle, but all around them the bodies of the slain littered the streets. The orcs stalked closer to the site of the battle's beginning, crossing the corpse filled town square and heading further into town. They soon came face to face with the survivors of the vicious fight.

A small number of orcs sat against the wall of a ruined building, talking with an even smaller group of trolls. They looked up as Ma-Gur and his two warriors approached. They were weary, but Ma-Gur could still see the thrill of victory in their eyes. They had defeated an enemy force nearly two thirds larger than themselves. By Ma-Gur's return they could surmise that the supply wagons were also theirs, so despite their heavy losses victory was theirs.

They were pitifully few in number, yet chose to take their rest in the open fields around the city, uncaring of the danger of such a decision. Around the wagons ragged bedrolls had been unfurled, upon which laid the sleeping warriors. A lone sentry had been posted, primarily to run off any carrion or wolves that strayed too close to the makeshift camp. The cries and howls of such scavengers rang out into the empty night was more than enough to keep the watchman from falling into slumber.

The ruins of the village were full of activity in spite of the lifelessness of those humans, orcs, and trolls present. In fact, these lifeless occupants were the reason for the activity. Carrion birds swooped down upon fallen soldiers, cawing and screeching as they picked at dead flesh. Wild dogs and pack of wolves fought their own battles over the meat in a strange parody of the struggle that had led to this veritable feast.

Though considered by the majority of the world to be cold and fearless, even by themselves, many of the warriors could not find rest. The sounds of the scavenger's feeding frenzy kept them awake. Experienced warriors could sleep anywhere and through anything it was said. Many now found that statement lacking. They had all killed and fought before, all were hardened veterans in their own ways. Yet they were primarily raiders, warriors who fought while on the move. This was the first time any of them had remained on the field of battle once the fighting and looting was done. They felt acid biting of fear and doubt, a sinister questioning that drilled its way into their thoughts. What more was a man, than eventual meat for others?

Upon awakening quite unrefreshed the warriors loaded their spoils onto the carts and began the journey in the last known direction of the horde's passing.

Chapter 10

Things were not going well for the horde. Ghalik cursed under his breath as he ran alongside his warriors, the group of greenskinned creatures running down the slopes of the gorge. In the last few days the raiding had turned sour. Villages were becoming more heavily fortified as the threat of the horde grew with the telltale smoke pillars that told all who could see that yet another piece of civilization was burning.

The number of villages and townships that supplied the dwarven stronghold with most of its food and wood had been more than halved. The horde had been moving fast, pillaging with an almost desperate haste, leaving burning ruins behind them as they poured over the land. Ghalik had hoped that the sudden appearance of the rampaging horde would stir the slow burning warfires of the stone men. He had gotten his wish, but it came in a form much different than he had expected.

Instead of one plodding army of hundreds of dwarves, the old wizard found himself fighting skirmishes with smaller yet more mobile forces. His plan of out maneuvering the dwarven army and entering the fortress behind them had dissolved into a full-scale brush war with many different groups of dwarven troops, and the numbers of his horde were dwindling. Apparently the villagers and dwarves had a contingency plan for such events. The villages could be seen with prefabricated and hastily erected defenses. Their garrisons aided by the appearance of even more dwarven troops.

Ghalik had sent a runner to the southern orc clans in hopes of reinforcement even before he had set out on this campaign and left Ma-Gur's ill-fated forces behind, but the likelihood of both the runner's survival and a favorable response from the Angir's stooped counterparts was slim. Perhaps if they had also suffered the attacks of the dwarf and elf aided crusaders the southern orcs would come, but it was an inconsequential thing. Ghalik had the immediate situation to deal with.

Two regiments of dwarven shock troops had used their superior familiarity with the terrain to outmaneuver the horde, trapping them at the bottom of a gorge. Even now as Ghalik looked on the dwarven regiments came at them, one from each end of the gorge. In such narrow confines the horde would not be able to escape, and if the fight lasted for too long one of the other dwarven companies that scoured the land might have the chance to join in. It seemed as if their time was at an end.

With a grunt of resignation Ghalik raised his waraxe and began to chant the language of magic. The stalwart dwarven column continued to march towards the waiting horde as tendrils of energy began to creep along the shaft of the wizard's axe. Never the sort to wait for a fight to come to them, the trolls bellowed their war cries and followed Reygoth in a charge against the oncoming line of dwarves. The knot of troll warriors crashed into the dwarven ranks, Reygoth's greatsword cutting a bloody swathe as he waded into the enemy. Despite their initial losses the robust dwarves bravely met the charge with axe and hammer.

First a trickle, then a flood of orcs began to follow suit. Rushing into the fray, partly out of bloodlust and impatience, partly because they knew and feared Ghalik's magic. Thus the company of dwarves steadily marching towards the center of the gorge found themselves facing only the orcish wizard and Ca'tic'na's goblins.

Ghalik's eyes glowed with a sickly green light as he finished the arduous spell. The sounds of combat rang in his ears, but he heard only the rush of energy as it coursed through his body. He voiced a great bestial roar and swung his glowing axe at the ground directly in front of him. When the blade bit into the gorge floor a loud boom sounded, and the ground in front of the wizard shook with an unfathomable force. The power of the earthquake spell brought the vast majority of the marching dwarves to the ground.

The goblins, whose cowardice was dissipated by the sight of so many fallen enemies, rushed forward like a swarm of giant insects. Their spears and shortswords claimed many dwarven lives before the stout warriors were able to fight back. By that time Ghalik himself slammed into them. Like an army unto himself he laid about him with the waraxe, still crackling with energy and now slick with smoking blood.

Okada and Ma-Gur reached the slopes of the gorge just as Ghalik's earthquake spell felled the dwarves on that end of the gorge. The large orc warrior had been met by the smaller ranger while on his way towards the horde. Okada had told him of the unforeseen dwarven tactic, and to consider himself lucky he hadn't run afoul of any patrols on his way to the horde. The two of them had led their forces to the gorge in an attempt to turn the battle in their favor. They watched as Ghalik slaughtered the dwarven shock troops, yet they could see that the old wizard was wounded many times over and getting weaker.

"Okada, you and your goblins do what you can for Ghalik. I will finish the dwarves on the other end," stated the large orc. At the commanding tone Okada initially bristled but could see the determination and confidence in Ma-Gur's eyes, so chose not to argue.

"Then I'll meet you in the middle," Okada uttered as he signaled his goblins to him and unslung his stolen elvish bow.

As Okada rained down arrows with terrifying accuracy his goblins moved down the slope. Once they were in range they hurled their spears into the dwarven ranks and charged with shortswords at the ready. The dwarves were sufficiently distracted by the surprise assault that their unified assault on Ghalik lessened. Within moments that end of the gorge was a jumble of the two groups of goblins and the dwindling numbers of dwarves. Having loosed all of his arrows, Okada bound down the slope with sword in hand. Ghalik fought on. Freed from the press of enemies, he was more able to choose his targets and conserve his power.

Ma-Gur sprinted back to where his warriors waited, impatient for battle.

"Bring the weapons cart around. Take it to the edge of the slope," Ma-Gur commanded as he signaled for his warriors to follow him, "We are going to let the wagon run down the slopes before us."

At in inquisitive glance from a nearby orc Ma-Gur made his intentions clear.

"I mean to use the cart as a battering ram. It will break their ranks and allow us to get close to them. Now move!" he bellowed as the group approached the far slopes.

The remaining trolls under Ma-Gur's command held the cart poised over the edge, pointed at the tight dwarven ranks. This regiment seemed much larger than the one Ghalik faced, yet as Ma-Gur looked on he was able to see that a third dwarven force had moved in to back up the first group, which had sustained heavy causalities yet held its ground. At Ma-Gur's signal they heaved the wagon over the edge, the force of their shove sending the cart careening down the slopes towards the dwarves. Following quickly behind the descending makeshift battering ram the orc and troll warriors rushed down into the gorge to aid their comrades.

The dwarves never saw it coming. Without warning the heavy cart full of weapons and armor crashed into the tight ranks of the dwarven soldiers. The short warriors were thrown in every direction as the wagon broke over them, sending its cargo of edged metal in every direction as a hapless dwarf was caught in the spokes. The cart broke into several pieces as it flipped end over end before it landed, damaging even more dwarves. Into the gap that was now formed in the dwarven formation poured the descending orc and troll killers. The dwarf line crumbled under the pressure of the two groups of warriors.

Soon the sounds of battle died away as the few dwarves that had survived finally made their escape. The horde had suffered, and was now collectively no more than a strong raiding party in number. Ghalik, weary and wounded, was angry and disappointed. The horde had paved their way down the mountains to the dwarven stronghold with their own lives, only now to be far too few to finish the game. They had marched through army after army and village after village, at least the knowledge of their bloody path was a small comfort. While they could not capture the stronghold, they could always sell their lives against the dwarven regiments still afoot in the land.

Ghalik watched as Ca'tic'na and what remained of his goblins worked over the corpses like carrion. Picking out bits of trail rations, weaponry, and other wealth that only goblins could appreciate. His gaze fell upon the fiercely proud Reygoth, harvesting a dwarven skull for his banner, upon which already hung the skulls of several humans. Neither leader seemed to notice the penetrating look of the orc wizard. It seemed to Ghalik that they were proud and accepting of their roles and the situations in which they found themselves.

Ghalik thought perhaps it was for the best that his tribe was dying before his eyes. Mayhap the world would be a better place if loremasters like he and Ca'tic'na died out. The creatures of the world could go on living their lives without the terrible weight of history on their shoulders. Youth could not live their lives as they pleased, not that humans, orcs or any other race would choose to live any differently. Yet they could live without the bitter knowledge of the origins of their worlds. They could choose their paths without awareness of the dark purpose hiding in their blood.

Perhaps, unknowingly, that was why the humans, elves and dwarves seemed to flourish so. While the races of the trolls, goblins and orcs fell into decline. *That is why we are the ancient races*, Ghalik thought, *because the humans and their allies have forgotten their places whereas we have not.*

They are free in their ignorance and we are slaves to our knowledge. What if the ancient raced forgot their hatreds? What if they were to forget why they craved battle so? Would they weaken and die? No, he thought not. *They would thrive in their quest for answers, and still bring the might of the world against them in the end. It was best that tribes like the Angir died off, taking their loremasters and their secrets to the grave.*

But Ghalik was an orc, said by many to be what was best in orcs, and he was not about to lay down and die. He knew that his death and that of his people wouldn't save the orc race as a whole, but even if it did it wasn't a sacrifice he would have made. Suicide was the one taboo that was held in all orc tribes, leftovers from their deific heritage. No orc would sacrifice itself for another or take its own life out of misery or for honor. Ghalik did not intend to fail or die so cheaply. He would die hard and fast, taking as many of the enemy with him as possible.

The expectant looks from the warriors that had gathered near him told him the time for contemplation was over. They don't want speeches or lore, they want action. Ghalik, still in pain, stood.

"We are too few in number to assault the citadel. If we did we would waste our lives and accomplish nothing. It would be better to turn our might against the dwarven troops that still hunt for us, there at least we can do some damage," stated the weary wizard as the strapped his gory axe to his broad back.

"I have news Ghalik, that may change your mind," spoke Okada as he shouldered his way towards the front of the crowd.

"Go on."

"As you say, an assault on the citadel at our current strength would not succeed. Even though we discovered a side entrance to the stronghold. It is easy to enter, but unless the citadel could be taken quickly it would be difficult to defend," Okada explained as he looked from Ghalik to the assembled crowd, "Yet on my way here to the gorge I met runners from the southern tribes. They come to meet us. They travel with hordes from the east, who have also felt the blades of Iithsul. Their seers have told them that they must meet us at the gates of the citadel in two days time, so they run hard towards us. If we have taken the stronghold they will enter as friends, if not they will attack on their own."

"They are as wise as they are numerous. All know that to survive this purge we of the ancient races must take refuge behind walls. This is the nearest fortress of worth for hundreds of miles and far enough from the human cities and the elven forests that it can be taken and held," Ghalik said as he gave the signal to pack up and move out. "Then we have two days to get to the citadel and assault it. Let us hope that we can hold it long enough for our allies to arrive to save us."

No other words needed to be said. All knew that the plan was to use Okada's secret entrance to infiltrate the stronghold and attack it from within. The wagons were loaded with all that they could carry, and the dead were left for the scavengers. The small horde moved out swiftly before any more enemies arrived.

By the time two more dwarven companies crept into the gorge all that was left to greet them were the carrion-savaged bodies of the slain.

Chapter 11

The fortress of Ameran, dwarvish for The Mountain Tomb, had visitors.

Okada slid down the narrow passageway, his face and armor caked with ash and soot. He moved down the shaft, the treacherous hand holds of the vertical gap in the mountain threatening to give way under his weight. As a fresh wave of soot covered him from above he looked up at the upside down orc descending after him.

The silent threat in the ranger's eyes were enough to chasten Ma-Gur as he slowed his rapid descent. The ranger had said that there was a reliable way in, but he had no idea this was what he meant. An entrance maybe for goblins or the nimble ranger, but a difficult challenge for more bulky warriors like Ma-Gur. Yet they all descended just the same, at that point they really had little choice.

Ghalik had explained to the warriors that Okada had discovered a weakness in the dwarven defenses. Their smelteries and forges all required steam and soot removal systems, without them the foundries would soon be choked with steam and covered in ash and coal soot. Somewhere deep in the mountain dwarves had set up massive billows, an airbladder that when pumped could push the air up the mountain's natural vents. The rising air would carry most of the steam or soot out of the foundries and into the air outside.

As long as they were quiet and able to suffer the searing pain of the ash laden steam the small force would be able to penetrate deep into the mountain's fastness. It was the stealth part that was giving Ma-Gur so much trouble. Even though his body weight was supported by ropes from above, he found that finding a purchase on the soot-covered walls was exceptionally difficult. It didn't help that he was being forced to make the descent upside down. The blood was pounding in his head, yet he realized that he would be able to better navigate the vent by going down headfirst and thus make good time.

Okada came to a stop right at the end of the shaft, finding that it came out in the low ceiling at the center of the foundry. Below him a number of dwarves toiled blissfully with hammer and tong, crafting the metals that marked the peculiar genius of their race. Oblivious to the threat descending from above the haggard craftsmen continued with their work. Thankfully they did not notice the small piles of soot that had collected on the ground as a result of the climb down the shafts.

Okada gave a signal to the other warriors who had reached his level from the several other shafts in the ceiling. As Ma-Gur joined him, Okada and the other warriors began silently lowering themselves down the ropes towards the unsuspecting dwarves.

Ma-Gur stayed even with the other half dozen warriors who were descending in the first wave. Like the others, he picked a dwarf who was almost directly underneath him and closed in. The first wave of warriors had been instructed by Okada to use stealth blades. They were daggers that had been smeared with a mixture of spittle and ash, which dulled their shine so that no light would glint off the metal and give the dwarves a chance to notice and raise an alarm.

He lowered himself almost right on top of the dwarf, keeping just out of range of the heavy hammer the dwarf was using to beat a red-hot piece of edged metal. Had the smith looked up he would have seen a sea of red eyes staring down back at him. Yet his attention remained fixed on the metal, which to him was the very fiber of the world.

Ma-Gur waited until the hammer struck metal once more, then with blinding speed descended the last two feet and attacked the dwarf. The large orc reached out and wrapped one arm around the dwarf's throat and lifted him off the ground. With the other hand he plunged the stealth dagger deep into the dwarf's heart. The dwarf gurgled and tried to swing his hammer at his killer, but the blow fell short as Ma-Gur released his grip. The struggling dwarf fell to the ground and writhed in agony as his life seeped out onto the hot tiled floor.

Ma-Gur was about to uncoil his legs from the ropes and somersault to the ground on his feet when another dwarf charged him. Ma-Gur twisted his torso around just in time as the dwarf's hammer connected. The blow spun Ma-Gur away, his sword and shield knocked away from their place on his back as he flew through the air. Ma-Gur came swinging back as he saw the dwarf raising his hammer for another blow. It never landed, because as Ma-

Gur swooped in he released his grip of the rope with his legs, but held on with his hands. He used his momentum to flip his body around and plant both of his feet into the dwarf's chest with a rib-crushing dropkick that sent the dwarf sailing through the air.

The orc hurried to release himself from the rope as the sturdy dwarf shakily regained his footing. Ma-Gur had just managed to stand when the bleary eyed dwarf stumbled forward, clearly wounded but not defeated. The orc cast about in a desperate search for defense as the dwarf clumsily rushed him with hammer raised. At the last moment Ma-Gur cursed aloud and grabbed a half-formed weapon of heated metal and buried it's red-hot edge in the dwarf's skull. He released its burning handle as the pain became unbearable. His right hand had become quite useless.

He looked up to see that the other orcs had faired better for the most part. All of the dwarves in the foundry were dead, and with only two casualties. The rest of the horde descended into the foundry as the first wave secured the area. Ma-Gur bound his hand with cloth strips from a nearby workbench while he watched Ghalik order for the assault teams to form up.

Ma-Gur was part of the group that was to find its way to the gate and disable it from the inside. It was the largest of the three groups and led by Ghalik. They had to first find the gate, and then raise it. With that done they were to somehow disable the closing mechanism and hold the gate open at all costs. This would allow the approaching orc army to easily enter the fortress and aid in the fight within.

The other two groups had smaller numbers and less specific orders. Reygoth commanded a force comprised mostly of the remaining trolls who were to wander the citadel causing as much chaos as possible. It was hoped that they would distract and harrow the resistance efforts of dwarves who might seek to protect the gate. Ca'tic'na and the remaining goblins had been ordered to find the dwarven food caches and prevent the dwarves from poisoning or retreating with them. Ghalik surmised that even if victory in the citadel was achieved that they would soon find themselves under siege from other forces within weeks. The army needed that food, and who better to ferret it out than a pack of hungry goblins?

The three assault groups quickly formed up and got underway. Reygoth penetrating deeper into the mountain in search of dwarven adversaries with a certain gleefulness that trolls seemed to be overcome with right before battle. Ca'tic'na and his band slinked off into the shadows in search of the food stores. Ghalik gathered his troops to him and headed for the gate.

None of the invaders knew the layout of the fortress, but while dwarven architecture is elegant it is also quite simple. It was not very difficult for the invading groups to navigate through the underground fortress. After a short time of wandering Ghalik's group ran across a few sentries and quickly eliminated them. Soon the group came to a precipice that overlooked the convoluted workings of the massive gate.

Never in their long lives had they seen a mechanical creation of such magnitude and complexity. The only knowledge of architecture possessed by the orcs was the mildly complicated layouts of the towns and villages they repeatedly raided. Nothing of this sort had ever been witnessed by modern orcish eyes. Even Ghalik and some of the older warriors, all of who had been alive for many hundreds of years, had never witnessed anything quite so magnificent. Though, magnificent and strangely beautiful as it was, its elegance was lost on the orcish minds. They had not come to marvel, but to lay waste.

The bulk of the horde rushed down the staircase, hoping to engage the guards before they could put up any sort of formidable resistance. As the warriors rushed the small gatehouse Okada, whose newfound skill with a bow was alarmingly accurate, felled the two sentries positioned at the alarm bell. The surprised dwarves barely had time to raise their weapons in defense as they were overrun by the charging orcs.

Within moments the orcs had secured the gatehouse. They were about to congratulate themselves on their victory when a single loud note filled the air. All turned just in time to see Okada sink a second arrow into one of the sentries, but the orcish archer was too late to prevent the stout warrior from sounding the alarm. The dwarf slumped to the ground, dying with the comforting knowledge that his kinsmen could hear the bell and come to avenge his death.

"Hurry! We haven't much time 'til the stone men come back to claim their gate!" bellowed Ghalik as he gestured for the group to spread out, "We've got to get that gate open and hold it open!"

Ma-Gur and three other warriors rushed into the gatehouse to open the gate as the rest of the horde took up positions at the handful of doorways that opened up to staircases leading down to the gatehouse. Thankfully all of the doors came from either side of the gatehouse with the empty inner courtyard below them and the blank wall to which they had their backs.

Ma-Gur could see the courtyard out of the glassless window of the gatehouse. He gazed down upon the tremendous gate of wood and stone, a construct that no siege engine or battering ram could ever hope to break. His eyes traced the lines of chains and rope that raised and lowered the gate back to the gatehouse. Even with his primitive understanding of mechanics he could fathom the gate's operation. He only had to simply pull the one lever in the room to raise the gate. The dwarves after all had expected invasion from without, not within.

He realized after a few unsuccessful attempts that he would need help, so called over his three comrades. Together they pulled the lever backwards, with every inch they pulled the massive gate raised a foot. The grating sound was tremendous, and threatened to make their ears bleed with its racket. When the gate was raised all the way the sounds had not stopped. At first the orcs looked about in confusion, then suddenly realized that what they were hearing was not the gate, but the sound of fighting.

They rushed outside to discover that the dwarves had rallied and were trying to reclaim the gate. Orcs stood shoulder to shoulder at the doorways, desperately fighting off the endless numbers of dwarves that seemed to keep emerging from the bowels of the mountain. The three orc warriors made to join the battle, but Ma-Gur blocked their way with his considerable stature.

"We are the last line of defense. If one side breaks we will be all that stands between the stone men and the gate. We have to hold the gate for the coming clans," he ordered as he looked back at the last ditch efforts of the embattled and outnumbered orcs.

"And if the clans do not appear?" asked one of the warriors.

Ma-Gur turned slowly to face him and said, "Then we die alone."

It was not long until the dwarves had pushed Ghalik and his warriors back to the very threshold of the gatehouse. There were only a handful of orcs left by the time they were pushed back to Ma-Gur's position. Okada stood with the younger orc as they fought side by side, the ranger's arrows long ago spent. Ghalik's magic was all that kept them from being overrun. He had cast a spell on the area right in front of the gate house. It was a spell that slowed movement, and was managing to keep the dwarves from being able to mount an effective group charge. Yet the spell's power was fading fast as more and more dwarves moved into its area of effect, gradually sapping away its power and potency.

Yet, when all seemed lost, a terrifying chorus of inhuman howls filled the courtyard. Orc and dwarf alike turned to look upon the source of the sound. All were surprised when an army of orcs began to pour in through the gate. Though the Angir were the only known orcs to stand tall and possess hair, the stooped and wretched orcs of the southern and eastern clans numbered in the thousands. Like the myths and legends of old, they flowed into the citadel like a green tide of muscle and steel.

The dwarves, realizing that to close the gate now was a waste of time and lives, quickly ceased their assault of the ravaged group of orcs in the gatehouse and disappeared back into the bowels of the mountain fastness. No doubt they meant to engage the mind numbingly vast army now filling their citadel like water in a porous stone. It was hopeless they knew, but no dwarf intended to abandon his home without a fight.

With a sense of elation and awe the mere dozen survivors stepped out of the gatehouse and looked out into the courtyard. Orcs were still jostling their way into the fortress, by now there must be thousands filling the halls with blood and death. Still more poured through the gates, though now the steady stream had lessened to a trickle, until only sporadic clusters of stragglers joined the invasion.

As the Ghalik and his warriors looked on, two orcs walked in through the gates. They were both bedecked in bones and leather fringe, the marks of leadership in both the southern and eastern clans. They both had the look of killers, far beyond the prowess and capacity of the orcs they led. It could be seen in their movements, they were trained in the war arts like the Angir, not simply berserkers like the majority of other orcs. The dried blood and grisly trophies that hung from their belts told the story of the wars they must have fought to have come this far north through human and dwarf territories.

They looked up at Ghalik and raised their curved weapons in salute, one which was met by Ghalik's own upraised waraxe.

The battle for Ameran was won.

Chapter 12

Ma-Gur looked at his scarred hand intently, clenching and unclenching it as he watched the muscles play back and forth across his bones. The wounds burned into his hands by the hot metal weapon with which he had dispatched the dwarf still pained him, but it was a phantom pain of a wound long since healed. Though a warrior and a veteran of an increasing number of battles the pain from the wounds caught up with him at times. The burn had been large and deep, and though his orcish heritage bestowed him with accelerated healing, the memory of the horrible pain sometimes came to him. Even orc, it seemed, could not abuse their bodies without eventual consequences.

The sound of hammers ringing in the morning air caught his attention, bringing him roughly out of his reverie. His gaze followed the sound, carrying his vision beyond his perch atop one of the citadel's high sentry towers. Beyond the gates of Ameran lay the workings of a vast army. Just out of missile range the dwarves and men were constructing massive battlements. The sight took Ma-Gur's mind back through the events that had unfolded over the last few months.

Once the clans of the eastern and southern orcs had entered the castle, a massacre had ensued. The vastly outnumbered dwarves had stubbornly defended their stronghold, bringing death to many orcs even as they themselves were slain. Reygoth and the trolls were said to have been in the thick of it, having already been engaged with the hard-pressed defenders. Ca'tic'na and the goblins had been discovered holed up in the citadel's larder. Apparently they had penetrated the larder, killed the guards, and had been defending their position when the clan orcs stormed the halls.

Once the fortress had been taken Vol and Aar, the clan chiefs, had acquiesced leadership to Ghalik. While this had initially been ill received by the clan orcs, distrustful of their seer's submission to the leadership of another,

Ghalik quickly proved his leadership skills and secured his position. This was because within a week a large force of dwarves assaulted the citadel. The dwarves were unprepared for the sheer numbers of orc defenders or the discipline and fervor Ghalik had instilled in them.

After the dwarves had been routed and run down Ghalik had warned the victorious of over celebration or laxity in their vigilance. Soon, he had said, the armies of man, elf, and dwarf will arrive at our doorstep. They had to be prepared for the long and vicious battles ahead.

The gate had been closed. Defenses damaged during the orc occupation were repaired. Hunting and raiding parties scoured and ravaged the land for game and loot. Within a month most all of the nearby villages had been taken. The buildings had been torn down for raw materials, the larders plundered for food, and the populations dragged into the underground warrens as slaves.

After the second month had passed winter had set in. Soon Ghalik's wisdom was made clear to all. The overstocked food supplies promised a winter free from hunger. The mountains of scrap wood provided an abundance of warmth and fuel for the forges. The slaves provided ceaseless labor and service, allowing for the orcs to keep their war skills from being blunted by toil.

It was in the middle of the third month that the army came. They were led mostly by the knights and soldiers of Iithsul, yet the bulk of the army had the swarthy complexions of the warriors of Erol. Erol was a nation deep in the southern lands, famous for their mercenaries and their spicy cuisine. Apparently the coffers of mighty Iithsul were full enough to tempt the Erolite mercs to brave the winter and aid in the siege, that and their hatred of the ever-raiding southern orc clans who had escaped the purge. The company of dwarves that camped with the army indicated that the dwarves seemed to have gained the help of the humans. Who knew what they had offered in return.

Much to the defender's surprise the army had not made an assault. They had a different approach in mind. Without an aggressive movement at all the army set at once to building what appeared to be a massive set of ramparts that stretched from one end of the stronghold to the other.

It wasn't until the construction of the ramparts were well underway that Ghalik and his warriors realized the purpose of the project. The walls were built right up to the base of the mountain on either end of the stronghold in a crescent shaped semi-circle. They were just out of missile range and when completed would effectively hem in the orcs, trapping them in the mountain fastness.

Ghalik had pointed out that the enemy likely intended to starve them and whittle down their numbers. Since the horde's forces had not grown since the occupation of the dwarven citadel, other than the addition of a few small groups of trolls and goblins who appeared just before the siege began, there would be no help from outside.

So this is where fate has deposited us, thought Ma-Gur as he shivered against the cold. Under siege and trapped. Well, he though, at least the enemy has lost some of their initial patience. After a few weeks of bloodless siege the enemy, presumably spurred on by the dwarves, had begun to assault the stronghold. So despite the fact that the orcs detested siege warfare, they had their hands full repelling attacking troops and exchanging missile fire with enemy siege engines that moved up to support the troops.

It wasn't that the enemy had much of a chance of penetrating the fortress, but it did cost resources and lives to maintain the impregnability of the dwarven masterpiece. And a masterpiece it was, built long ago by the dwarves as a symbol of their mastery of stone and war, or so the legends told. The fortress was designed so that a scant few warriors could defend it as long as their supplies held. Which of course would soon be the problem given the thousands of warriors within the walls, not to mention the hundreds of slaves held below. It seemed the enemy's plan truly was to whittle them down into nothing.

Ma-Gur's eyes grew heavy, he had been on sentry duty for the better part of the day, and was eager for relief. As if on cue there was a tap on his boot, he looked down to find Okada and a clan orc standing below him in the stairwell.

"Ghalik has called for his leaders. Tonight he seeks a vision to save us," the ranger stated, "Be it from siege, or from boredom judging by your face."

Ma-Gur allowed himself a chuckle, which for orcs was about the extent of laughter and mirth. He never did understand Okada's sensibilities, seen as a weakness by others, but at times it amused the warrior. He joined Okada and descended the stairs as the stooped clan orc took up the sentry position behind them.

Ghalik gasped, the air about him thickened as the psychoactive drug began to take effect. His blood felt thick as his eyelids seemed to flutter in tandem with his rapidly beating heart. Ghalik's vision blurred and he began to feel as if he were growing lighter, his body feeling like it was slowly rising up from the ground. Through numbing lips he whispered in the broken language of magic, the energy coalescing about him as the spell began to take effect.

Those warriors present could feel the pull of the magical energy as it passed through them and into the old wizard. They were seated in a rough circle around the wizard, instructed by the seers Vol and Aar to remain still and silent no matter what happened.

The old orc began to convulse as he became fully enmeshed in the techniques of trance as taught to him by his fellow magicians, becoming the very device through which the spell of divination would manifest. The onlookers began to notice the brilliant sheen on his skin, a phosphorescent coat of sweat that flowed forth from his pours. Then, without warning his head flew back and he began to speak in a voice not his own.

"Down we must go. Into the Deep where the stone men fear to tread. A lifeline we must forge to the lands of the Sheul. Ruin has been laid upon our shoulders and it is Ruin we shall visit upon our oppressors. So it shall be until the end of our days."

The room fell silent as the Ghalik slumped to the floor unconscious. Grim looks were exchanged, the course was set. The future was unfolding even as they left the room, time speeding along its insane course through the abyss.

Chapter 13

"Surely we are spiraling towards the end my brother," Vol, the eastern chieftain, uttered as he and Ma-Gur toiled alongside the labor crews deep in the underground tunnels below the captured citadel.

"Aye, but I intend not to go alone," responded the younger, though larger, orc as he hefted a boulder out and away from the human digging crews, "And if Ghalik is right the weapon we will need to scourge this world is almost at our fingertips."

The two orc warriors went back to digging. The particular tunnel in which they toiled was one of dozens that had been worked into the mountain over time. Ma-Gur certainly hoped this tunnel was the one. According to Ghalik the dwarves had hidden the chamber beneath layer upon layer of brick and stone. *The score of other tunnels were fakes, so this one must eventually lead to pay dirt*, he thought.

After all, they had been digging for nearly one hundred years. Had it really been so long? Ma-Gur could barely wrap his mind around the idea. Then he thought of the tunnels themselves. Every one of them stretching and twisting on for miles, all sealed tightly and booby-trapped every inch of the way. The stone men were serious about keeping something hidden down there.

Ghalik had only hinted to the other orcs as to what lay beneath the century's worth of stone and sediment that had been moved. His only explanation for anything was that their prize was so valuable and terrible that the dwarves of olden times had built the fortress to keep whatever was buried there inside. How Ghalik knew this no one had a clue, and no one had the desire to ask. So here they were, nearly a century later, digging in the dark for some ancient evil.

At least life on the surface was interesting. The dwarves and men had finished their wall. A massive barricade of stone and wood bristling with siege weapons and archers. Ma-Gur assumed that the attackers had realized what the orcs were doing because over the last several decades the assaults grew more vicious and desperate. Perhaps the secretive stone men had finally told the humans what lie underneath the fortress.

Unfortunately for the attackers the orcs were a race of pitiless immortals, and so their numbers only dwindled through violent death. The dwarves had built their fortress well, and even after a century of siege, Ameran still stood defiant against the world that sought its end. In spite of the constant whittling of their numbers and the lack of conventional food supplies, the horde survived. The orcs had learned to cultivate the fungus that grew in the dark places of the underground. With Ghalik's foresight and Okada's practical wisdom, the orcs had managed to find the ways in which the dwarves survived within their mountains during times of war.

Without sympathy the orc horde used its original stock of slaves and bred them with captured soldiers before the invader's bodies were hung from the ramparts. After a hundred years of toil there were no human slaves left who had not been born into bondage deep in the mountain. Stones that came from the tunnels were hauled up and used for repairs and catapult ammunition. Fungal bodies that could be burned like wood were discovered in the catacombs. For all intents and purposes, Ameran was self-sustainable and impregnable. A living legend amongst the newest generation of besiegers and the various allied nations from which they hailed.

Ghalik, looking no older than he did a hundred years ago, breathed in the smoke from his wizard's incense. He contemplated the state of affairs in Ameran. The gridlock was beginning to wear thin. Of course the soldiers were unhappy. Though they often had much opportunity for battle, but it was siege warfare. Defending ramparts was tedious, and in every orc's heart of hearts open warfare was the only satisfying way to fight. The old wizard had heard talk of counter-assaults but had prevented them from occurring. Even Reygoth, a much older and slower creature these days, seemed to have lost his will to continue with affairs as they were.

Thinking of this, the old wizard opened his eyes to look at the old troll. Reygoth lay upon a crude cot, his mottled skin having lost its yellow luster of his younger days.

"You wear a long face old friend," croaked the troll as he noticed Ghalik's eyes upon him.

"Much has happened to give me grief. I have seen ages come and go like morning and night. This one is no different, yet I find myself unable to welcome its conclusion," mumbled Ghalik, embarrassed for such an unusual display of emotion.

"Perhaps it is the killing boredom that stalks this place. Before I was unable to stand even defending the walls grew tiresome. We long for the open fields and room to breathe or fight. I cannot imagine what it must be like to live out as many years as you have, only to be trapped in this tomb," the troll chuckled bitterly, "I at least have the luxury of dying before even death loses it's fire."

"The ancient races have lived our times in this world. All around us the world is changing. We have been left behind. Yet we still remain, caged like animals," Ghalik spat.

"Once you find the Sheul you will give the world one last glimpse of its origins before your time comes," coughed the troll as he rolled over to face the wall. "I know that an old crippled warrior like me has no business giving advise to an immortal wizard. But once you find what you seek, never, ever go back to this."

The troll weakly reached out and ran his hand down the dank wall next to his cot and whispered, "It will consume your spirit. As it has mine."

The troll's hand fell back to the cot. Ghalik looked at the troll's back for a long time. Then eventually rose to leave, a resolve growing in him that he had thought long dead.

"Thank you," he spoke softly, though his words fell on deaf ears.

Ma-Gur grunted and swung his pickaxe at the rock-filled wall of dirt in front of him. After a century of digging, he was by far the strongest and best-equipped orc for the job. He and the handful of orcs near his size worked alongside the human labor crews, clearing dirt and rock away while the goblins scampered about the newly formed tunnel searching for traps or clues as to the tunnel's true purpose. While few orcs had met their end in these catacombs, the death toll by dwarven traps upon the slave population was heavy and had to be guarded against.

The burly orc's arms shivered as the pickaxe struck something hard and unforgiving somewhere under the mound of dirt. Hearing the sound of the impact the goblins scurried over to Ma-Gur's position. He shoved the human slaves out of the way and helped the goblins as they all dug with their bare hands. Oddly enough the dirt gave way easily, as if it were strangely repelled by whatever lie just underneath the surface. They continued to clear dirt and rock away until they found that the hard surface had been a massive stone door.

Ma-Gur sent a pair of goblins running after Ghalik, and third skulked off on his own, presumably to inform Ca'tic'na of their discovery. While they were waiting, the orc and goblins finished clearing the last of the dirt from the door. Upon its surface was an inscription, presumably dwarvish. Ma-Gur couldn't read the script, but assumed that it told or warned of what lie behind the massive doors that stood slightly taller than the orc himself and seemed quite thick.

The goblin runners found Ghalik still standing in Reygoth's chamber, looking blankly at the last of the trolls. Hid mind burned with the knowledge that he had just witnessed the death of a race. Reygoth had confided in him many years ago that like the orcs the trolls had found themselves under attack, their women and children slaughtered as the troll clans were overrun by the vast armies of men. It was said that the High King of Iithsul had begun what he considered a holy crusade against the old races. Even though the cleric nation lay far to the south, the templars and soldiers had ranged even to the northern wilderness of the Angir. Surely after a century the High King had died, passing on his power and position to the next holy man.

"Time moves ever faster. The end speeds towards us in the swiftness of the passing days. Every year seems a day. Every life sparkling only a moment," he intoned as the goblins entered the room.

They told him of Ma-Gur's findings in their strange language, gesturing this way and that. Ghalik instructed one to lead him to the tunnel and the other to find Okada. Within minutes they had reached the catacombs. After moving down the tunnel for several miles deeper into the mountain they finally emerged into the small chamber carved out around the great stone door. Without words he stepped up to the door and began to run his hands over the dwarven inscriptions, murmuring to himself in a strange language that could only have been dwarvish.

Okada arrived shortly after, closely followed by Ca'tic'na and Aar. They joined Ma-Gur and Vol to watch in silence as Ghalik stood before the door. After many long moments the old wizard spoke to them over his shoulder as he traced his finger over an especially bizarre symbol at the center of the door.

"Imprisoned within this chamber is one of the Sheul, Lord Arius," he stated as he turned around to face his commanders, "This is a god from the ancient world, somehow captured by the stone men and held by old magics. This is the weapon I have promised you. Even as we are the ancient race, this

Sheul was the oldest of titans."

Then, without the slightest pretense, he turned and heaved against the great door. His muscles strained, but did not seem to be able to budge its fastness. Vol, Aar, and Ma-Gur shouldered past the goblins and added their strength to the wizard's. As they grunted and strained the door began to move, folding inwards as the orcs forced it open.

They found themselves in a large chamber. It was circular in shape, and in alcoves all around the chamber there were piles of black armor and weapons. There was enough armor and weaponry to equip a massive army. At the center of the chamber was a throne, its black metal frame bedecked with spikes and blades. Seated upon the throne was a massive suit of armor.

The form upon the throne would have stood just as tall as Ma-Gur, its bizarre armor adding bulk to its already large frame. At its hands lay an axe and sword, wicked weapons that had seen countless ages of bloodshed. In the center of its breastplate was an impression in which it seemed a circular stone or key should fit.

The crypt was silent as death as the orc commanders walked slowly into the room. As they approached a booming and sinister voice sounded in their minds.

"So my children have come to free me at last," spoke a voice so ancient it threatened to crush those who heard it.

Ghalik and the others stood at the base of the raised throne. Ghalik gathered his courage and spoke.

"Lord Arius, last of the Sheul. I have heard your voice in my dreams Old One. We have come to bring you into an age of war."

The visor of the great helm that sat atop the armored shoulders of the creature began to glow from a source deep within the metal shell.

"I am the last Sheul, the progenitor of orcish kind. Your strength is my power. Listen my children, and learn the last wisdom of the ancient world," it spoke as the orc commanders behind Ghalik were compelled to drop to one knee. Ghalik himself was in a trance and could not find the will to move, "Long ago I spawned your kind. The dwarves and the elves rallied to stop me from destroying this world. Your ancestors were sundered and scattered to all corners of the world. The other Sheul had been destroyed in our great conflict with the gods. Then I, Lord Arius, the First Orc, was defeated. An alliance of dwarven craftsmen and elvish sorcerers bound me with great magics. They forged my essence into this darksteel suit of armor that you see before you. The dwarves were then able to physically hold me here, while the elves hold the rune key that binds me to this throne."

"Ghalik, my last true son. You and your kin have become the killing spirit that will set me free. Find the rune key, return it here and I will stand at your side," the armored figure uttered in their minds as it turned up its palm. The movement was slight, but the grinding of the armor betrayed the difficulty of the movement, the god truly was held fast, "Send me the blood of your blood, and I will bless him so that he will be able to pass unseen into the kingdom of the elves."

Without a word Ghalik walked over to Okada and touched his shoulder. As the others looked on confused, Okada stood up next to the old wizard. The Ghalik removed an armored bracer from his wrist, revealing a strange tattoo. Every Angir orc bore a tattoo marking it as the child or kin of every other orc bearing that tattoo. Okada had been raised believing that his father had died in battle long ago. The mark on Okada's wrist was an exact copy of the one of Ghalik's own wrist. Then the truth hit all present like a hammer on steel, Okada was a superb ranger and warrior, but possessed no magic. Ghalik had hidden his heritage from the tribe to protect his son. All knew that if the Ghalik sired a son with no magic, it was to be put to death immediately for fear that it would sap the strength of the current Ghalik. A lifetime of forbidden emotions played over the muscles in Ghalik's face, and all could plainly see that it had sapped strength from the mighty orc. The greatest hero of their race, a traitor to even his own tribe, was truly the son of a deceitful god.

The old sorcerer said nothing, but simply gestured for the ranger to approach the throne. Okada visibly swallowed his confusion, fear, emotion, and stepped towards the armored creature. The thing remained still, though a palpable aura of power could be felt radiating from it. The ranger gingerly put his hand in the god's. There was a flash of magical energy, and then all was silent.

"Now I will await your return. Then I will stand with you at the end of ages."

Chapter 14

Merric looked out across the no man's land towards the citadel. He was a young archer from Erol, this was his first post as a mercenary. In the hundred years that the siege had gone on, the warriors of Erol had taken to sending fresh recruits to earn their place among the veteran companies by manning the walls against the orcs. The siege has escalated in the last few decades, the dwarves had made it clear to the human commanders that the fortress needed to be breached. The orcs were trying to raise some dead god or something, but that had been many years ago. Nothing had happened so far, but dozens of failed assaults against the impossibly defended citadel.

The orcs had never sallied forth from their fortress, so men like Merric had never faced orcs on the open field. Everything was siege warfare, so the young archer was caught unawares as the spear punctured his windpipe. He managed a gurgle before rough hands hauled him over the side.

Ca'tic'na was getting old. He could feel the muscles in his legs protesting as he vaulted over the lip of the battlement and onto the sentry's foothold. Goblins were longer lived than the trolls, but not by much. Only a few dozen goblins remained, the old warriors who represented the last of the goblin race. They had all insisted on accompanying Okada on his mission. What goblin, no matter how old and weak, wouldn't jump at the chance to penetrate the elven kingdom to attack it unawares?

The small band quickly swarmed over the wall, as goblins were notorious for not being impeded by such things as walls or barricades. Their small, clawed hands carried them up the sheer face of the barrier, then they quietly lowered a rope for the less able orc ranger. A few more guards were quickly dispatched as the force moved quietly along, making a stealthy dash for the tree line. The besiegers had grown lax over the last ten decades, and the warriors were able to easily eliminate the last remaining sentries and steal away from the camp.

They ran as fast as their legs could take them. It was only moments before a cry went up from the camp, proof that other guards had found their slain comrades. Mercenaries and horsemen quickly rode into the night to search for the assassins, but the ancient warriors had long since escaped them.

For nearly a week Okada and the goblins traveled hard. The lands they traveled through were new and fresh. Ca'tic'na had grown up raiding and pillaging most of these lands, and now he could hardly see a wall or even a presentable fence. In the century that the horde had been contained the world had become fat and lazy. *Such was the way of the new world*, thought the aging goblin. *Though we yet live, the world has all but forgotten us.* While the thought chilled his very soul, it did make him realize that their travels would be made easier by the slackness in the vigilance of this new age.

They eventually journeyed out of Ca'tic'na's homeland and came to the great river Thanos. It was known that the river flowed straight through the heart of the elven kingdom on its way to Erol. They slipped into a small river town under the cover of night and stole several of the villager's canoes. Soon they were speeding down the river towards their goal, Averinya, the elven nation city.

As they followed the river into the night they came to a great forest, the obvious boundaries of the elven nation. The raiders moored their boats and continued deep into the forest on foot. They had no doubts that many archers guarded the wood, yet oddly none came. They neared the city after two days in the woods, all with no sign of the elves. The Sheul's magic must have been tremendously powerful to keep them hidden so well and for so long.

Okada guided the goblins as they crept into the beautiful tree city, something in the back of his mind seemed to be guiding them. He seemed to know the exact moment in which to hide and where to do it when elven citizens and warriors crossed their path. He knew instinctively that the Sheul must have been guiding him, helping him towards the rune key. Oddly enough he found that he had a picture of it in his mind, without even having seen it, and he felt it drawing near.

Olisande Lostris, the king and high wizard of the elves, had been having fitful nightmares for nearly two weeks. This morning was no different as the started awake in a cold sweat. He quickly dressed, and to his surprise found himself strapping on his royal blade. *How odd*, he thought, *that I should dress for war when my only purpose today is music and reflection.* Olisande was old for an elf, a race that lived lives of beauty and grace for nearly as long as goblins, the accursed creatures. Elves would have others believe that they were descended from divine parents, alas, that was a lie told to greedy warriors and politicians who might raze the great elven city did they know otherwise.

Olisande was removed from his reflections as a warning bell could be heard in the distance. He grasped his sword and rushed to the source. From the tone and pitch of the individual bells he could discern that something was afoot in the vaults. As he ran through the palace towards them his archer captain, Torin Sic, joined him.

"My liege, the servants spoke of a horde of goblins attacking the vault. I rang the bells, but I fear we may be to late," Torin Sic breathed as they sped towards the vaults, a group of hand picked warriors joining them.

"Torin you take the palace guard into the vaults, eliminate any enemies you find there. I must go to the seer's tower, I fear greater evil is afoot here than mere robbers," commanded the elven king as he turned and ran up a nearby flight of stairs.

Torin Sic and his men reached the vaults shortly after. They found the bodies of several guards amidst a pile of goblin corpses. Torin knew that the only goblins left in the world were those of that cursed black citadel Ameran. If they were here it could only mean that they had discovered what evils lie beneath the mountain.

His men fanned out as they entered the vault, a long rectangular corridor full of pillars and doors set in the walls. The torches that usually illuminated the vault had been extinguished, though both goblins and elves could partially see in the dark. The elves spread into a fan formation and moved into the corridor like a wave. As they swept into the room the goblin robbers materialized out of the darkness. A battle, fast and fierce, erupted as the elves fired their deadly arrows and the goblins flung their barbed spears. As the two sides exchanged fire they closed in on each other, drawing wicked daggers and curved shortswords.

The elves were eager to slay the goblins, the chance of being the warriors to slay what must be the last of the goblin race was too personal to be left up to missile weapons. The goblins, their hatred for the elves burning brightly in their hearts, rushed to battle. They were the last, and intended to die clutching the souls of their most bitter enemy. Ca'tic'na hurled his spear into a nearby archer, who fell clutching her midsection. The old goblin drew his curved shortsword and charged the elf nearest him, a leader by the look of him.

Torin Sic fired an arrow into a goblin, then found himself under attack at close range. The elf captain dropped his bow and backpedaled as he drew his two knives to parry the flurry of blows that came from his shorter opponent. He was an immaculate bladesman, and only suffered a small cut to the leg before he made his move. Once he had both knives at the ready he suddenly halted his retreat, planting his feet firmly on the ground. With a flick of his wrist he turned his blade over from a parry to a slash, his blade slicing deep into the goblin's wrist. The smaller warrior lost his grip on the weapon and was unable to parry the second knife as the elf dragged its sharp edge across the goblin's throat.

As the goblin fell to the ground clutching his throat, Torin, his head throbbing feverishly for some reason, looked about him. The battle had ended. He and Eravin, a female archer, were the only survivors. He quickly sheathed his blades and retrieved his bow, knocking an arrow as he stepped forward. So many elves dead, but at least all of the goblins had perished. Eravin flanked him to the left as they picked their was through the battlefield towards the end of the vault.

They moved silently, keen eyes searching for hidden enemies. Eravin risked a glance across the hall at Torin Sic, just to make sure he was still with her. When she turned her head back her vision came to rest upon a shorter than usual orc, one that was pointing a stolen elvish bow in her direction. She quickly raised her bow, but her shot went wide as the orc fired his own arrow first.

Torin Sic heard the clatter of the missed shot and the double twang of two bows being fired. He turned to look at Eravin only to see her body collapse to the ground, a wicked black arrow buried in her heart. He took a step into the main corridor, but drew back instinctively just in time to evade another arrow aimed at him. The arrow ricocheted off a nearby pillar with a sharp crack, then the room again fell into silence. His vision was getting blurry and his body felt slow.

The elf slipped from pillar to pillar, listening intently for the tell tale sounds that would betray the enemy's position. Was it a goblin? Some little assassin missed during the earlier fight? His head jerked as he heard the scuffle of a boot on the hard pavement. He pulled back the string of his bow, trying to draw a bead on his shadowy opponent. There was a flicker of motion to his left, for an instant he saw the red eyes of his quarry, and though his own eyes were getting hazy, he fired.

He knew he had missed, now he was sure that the cut on his leg was poisoned, but at least he was driving his quarry into the open. He spun around, stepping around the other side of the pillar and into the main corridor. His enemy did the same. They stood facing each other, arrows poised for flight. Then Torin Sic realized it wasn't a goblin. It was an orc! They didn't have rangers! He paused in momentary confusion, the poison slowing his mind as it coursed through him.

That was his fatal mistake. Okada's arrow thudded into Torin's breast with enough force to knock him back. Torin dropped his bow and fell to his knees, his mouth open in shock. The ranger advanced as he drew back another arrow, the rune key glittering on a makeshift necklace at his throat.

In the seer's tower, Olisande screamed as he looked from the dead seer to the glowing visage of the Sheul in the cracked scrying mirror.

Chapter 15

"Now we are at the cusp of our doom!" bellowed Ghalik as he looked out from his raised dias at the last horde of orcs, "Once we open these gates there is no going back. We are the last of our kind, there will be no more who will come after. This is the first day of our extinction."

He clenched his fist and growled, "The men of Iithsul began a crusade against the ancient world. The trolls and goblins have already fallen, now it is down to us. Yes, we are immortal and have proven that we can live under siege. But we are orcs! We do not cower behind walls! As you have seen and felt yourselves, this place destroys our will. I say when we sally forth from this place that we never return to its safety. We must take our will and drive it into the heart of the world until we draw our last breath!"

The chamber was silent. No one dared speak. It was as if they could feel the power of the sorcerer and the newly awakened god pulsing through the citadel itself. Ghalik looked directly into Ma-Gur's eyes. The younger orc could see the Gor-Angir hiding in the wizard's eyes. In those eyes he saw the doom of he and his kind. The ancient world is ancient because it has come and gone, orcs were no longer meant for this place. So let the world burn.

Ma-Gur felt his blood boil. He held his sword and shield above him, thrusting them in the air, and roared. His single deep voice echoed through the empty halls of Ameran. An instant later thousands of voices answered his blood call, and the horde rushed to the walls.

Ma-Gur waited on the battlements, his breath slowed as the tried to calm himself. It was these moments of waiting that were the worst. Ghalik was right, a century inside those walls had sapped their strength. But now, now they had a god.

Okada had returned, ruined and wounded by his journey, but in possession of the rune key. True to its word the Sheul had been freed. When Okada ascended the steps like some returned messiah all had seemed right and powerful. Then the ranger had placed the rune key into the chest socket on the Sheul's armor. Almost instantly the ranger was disintegrated. Ghalik has set his jaw against the loss of his hidden son so hard that his lips bled, but like a true orc his heart hardened even as the blood ran over his chin and spilt onto the floor.

"This is the price for my return," its had said to Ghalik, "After all I am one of the sources of your being. You of all orcs should understand betrayal. Now he and I are one, his power is now mine."

Then the god turned to the gathered orcs and Ghalik's remaining commanders, "And so let us begin the end."

Bringing us here, thought the burly orc. The Sheul had armed them with the darksteel weapons and armor from his tomb. Enchanted yet cursed, whispered the metal to the warriors as they made ready for battle. The besieging army had been warned by the elves that the god had been brought back. Now they stood, rank upon rank, awaiting the coming fight. They had no idea, these fools of war, what the god had in store for them.

Everyone tensed as the gates of the citadel opened and spewed forth the Sheul, Lord Arius.

The ground trembled as Lord Arius strode into no man's land. His armored form hovered over the ground as it moved towards the enemy forces. The men of Erol, Iithsul, and dwarves huddled in their barricades as the dead god drew near.

Lord Arius held his weapons aloft and began to chant in the language of magic. Hearing what could only be the beginning of a spell the archers began to fire. Their arrows flew far and true, but they disintegrated as they struck his armor. His weapons began to glow along with his armor as his powers began to manifest. He spread his arms wide as a blast of pure energy arched out from him, destroying the enemy in waves. Then, as if the mass destruction was a signal in and of itself, Ma-Gur lead the orc hordes in a ferocious charge.

They reached Lord Arius just as he collided with the shattered enemy lines. Were his weapons fell men died by the dozens, only to have their comrades slain as the orcs followed in the god's wake. Within moments the battle had become a route, then the route a massacre.

And so it came to pass that the ancient world escaped from its prison of stone. Once more the past came forth to lay waste to the future. From the hill countries of Ameran, to the southern marshes of Erol, through the elven city and all the way to the nation of Iithsul, the horde burned and slaughtered. More quickly than any could have imagined, darkness covered the land.

Chapter 16

At the sound of their Lord's inhuman bellow, the horde began the assault. The final crusade against the templar nation that had first driven them underground had begun. Their howls were deafening.

But the opposition tonight was not the ordinary sort of adversary. These were the men of Iithsul, their phalanx of pikes gleaming in the torchlight like the faith burning brightly in their spirits. Not used to fighting at night, the warriors of Iithsul had set torches every ten paces across their battle line. Lights to illuminate no only the darkness of night, but to dispel the fear of facing the forces of the old world at long last.

The reports and rumors said that the orcs were lead by some sort of orc wizard who commanded a god thought long dead. They carried with them blades of darksteel, a metal forged deep in the ancient citadels of the Sheul, where all fear to tread. Darksteel was harder and lighter than most other metal, making it highly valuable. It also seemed to be unaffected by magic, prayer, or wards. However, legend held that to wield darksteel was to invite the powers of ruin into one's life.

High King Eldin, the current mortal vicar and representative of the great god Harrikan, pondered these things as he watched the advance of the massive army. He was large for a human, his height and strength testament to his god's favor. Some who had seen him at a distance even claimed that he had a shimmering halo about him, as if his body radiated the potent cleric's powers with which he was vested.

Atop his great steed he sat, resplendent in his white armor and cloak. *Soon,* he thought, *these beautiful garments will be soiled with blood. What a waste. It seemed that no matter how many battles were fought or how many years went by, there was always evil in the land.* He was not foolish enough to think good could exist without evil, but being a Hero and a good man he often found it difficult to accept that fact in his heart. So it was with a burdened sigh that he drew his sword, a blade so holy that none but him seemed able to wield it, and ordered his troops forward to defend their homes and their world.

The phalanx of pikemen began to march steadily forward, supported from the rear by rank upon rank of dwarven shock troops and human men at arms. Normally there would be deadly volleys of arrows raining down upon the enemy from elvish bows, but none fell today. The elves were gone, their race wiped out by Lord Arius and his horde. The elf's enchanted forest was now nothing but ashes, burned by the orcs and their wizard. So now only dwarves and men stood in the way of this ancient evil.

Yet the elves had not given up life easily. They had miraculously repelled the horde's first assault, the powerful magics of Olisande Lostris keeping the Sheul at bay. But then the orcish wizard and Lord Arius combined their sorcerous might to set fire to the elven forests. Soon the unquenchable flames had consumed both forest and city, driving the elves into the open. When the graceful warriors and their families fled the fires and came into the fields surrounding the forest they found themselves in an impossible situation.

The horde had built a shield wall that protected them from the arrows of the elves and still be able to hurl spears and get in close quarters without being filled with elven arrows. And so on the fields before the burning forest the elf race met its end in battle against the orcs and their powerful god. Olisande Lostris, or so the visions sent by Harrikan to Eldin during meditation revealed, fell in single combat against Lord Arius. As the High King watched Olisande opened himself to a deathblow from the Sheul in order to close in for a fatal strike himself.

But as Arius's blade rent the elf's body, Olisande's blade only cleaved the rune key in the god's breastplate. The High King watched as the elfking died in shock. As the Sheul looked up, obviously sensing the High King's scrying, Eldin realized that Olisande had failed to kill the god. Yet by destroying the rune key the elf had reduced the Sheul's power considerably, and more importantly bound it to the physical plane. Now it could be killed.

Eldin thought on this as the two armies finally met, their battle lines crashing into each other like waves against cliffs. The bloodthirsty orcs hurled themselves upon the pikes of Iithsul with suicidal courage and faith in their cursed armor. As those unlucky enough to be impaled crawled down the shafts to attack the pikemen themselves, the rest of the horde closed distance.

Too late, the pikemen realized the tactic. As the orcs died or whose armor deflected the points the pikemen began to lose both their weapons and advantage as the dying warriors clutched the poles to them, allowing those behind to gain ground. The pikemen's line broke as the steady waves of orcs washed over them. Those who had the chance dropped their now useless pikes and drew their daggers, trying desperately to stay alive while falling back. As the pikemen's retreat turned into a slaughter the dwarven shock troops and human men at arms waded into the fray. The orcs kept coming.

They came screaming bestial cries of fury as they rushed towards the warriors of the alliance. Man and dwarf alike felt the acid bite of fear as the muscular savages bore down on them. By now every one had heard the legends springing up on the crest of the horde's rampage. They were immortal beings spawned by the dark gods when the world was young. They reproduced in vast numbers and quickly grew into maturity. The only check on their numbers was their innate love, almost obsession, with violence and plunder. They respected and revered the mighty, so their only religion was the worship of battle and those who excel in it.

Now they were armed with blades of darksteel and had the patronage of a god enfleshed. In their brutal rampage they had managed to lay waste to most of the known world. Only the gilded towers of holy Iithsul remained unsullied. The one remaining light in this time of darkness and woe.

It was with that knowledge that the dwarves and men were able to stand firm and face the furious onslaught of the orcs. With the conviction and strength of desperation and hope they met the charge of the orcs with one of their own.

High King Eldin closed his eyes with sorrow as the two forces met. He could never shut out the sound of that initial clash. The bestial roars of the orcs mingled with the war shouts of man and dwarf as blades met and blood began to spill.

The fighting was thick and fierce. The orcs spurred onwards by their lust for battle, hacking and hewing even as they themselves were cut down. Men at arms fought desperately for their lives and the dwarves fell into a frenzy much like the orcs as they lost themselves in their ancient hatreds for the enemy.

Reserves were marched in from Iithsul to feed the battle with fresh lives. The casualties on both sides mounting as the night wore on. From time to time the pitch of battle would lessen as forces reformed, only to proceed into battle once again. Even a large force of unarmored commoners came from the city to fight alongside the others, armed only with farming tools and the desire to defend their homes.

Gradually the forces of darkness began to give ground. However, even as they fell back the Sheul revealed itself. Clad head to toe in black platemail, it brandished wicked weapons as it charged towards the battle.

It was that moment for which the High King had waited. With a shout he lead his mounted knights into battle. As the brilliant column of mounted knights drew near the thick of the fighting they moved to intercept the dark god who was cutting a bloody swathe through the ranks of the alliance. The closely packed combatants parted like a sea before the advance of the mounted troops.

Their collision was like the thunder of a thousand storms as the mounted warriors plowed into the armored giant. Blade and bludgeon crashed into shield and breastplate as the heavily armored combatants exchanged blows. For a time the struggle seemed evenly matched as the momentum of the mutual charge slowed and the struggle became mingled with the larger battle at hand.

Soon the High King found himself putting orcs to the sword as he tried to reach Lord Arius. Eldin's holy sword cut through normal metal as if it were barely there, yet the darksteel blades did not shatter. Thus the High King found that killing a foe that could parry without losing his weapon was more difficult than he was used to. However, High King Eldin was no normal man, he was a Hero. His blade took life after life, spilling more blood than the King cared to remember. It was then that he cut down a charging orc and made himself a clear view of Lord Arius.

The black armored Sheul, despite the loss of his destructive magics, was sowing death all about him. The dark god stalked about the battlefield lashing out with both axe and sword, killing as he went. Often he would severe a limb or disembowel an opponent, then move on, knowing the wound would eventually kill them and not wasting his time dealing out clean deaths. Lord Arius was a cold and calculating creature, every movement ended a life.

Perhaps it was this coldness that gave pause to the High King, or the fact that most of the templars were dead at it's feet, their loyalty and devotion carrying them straight to their deaths. For a moment all Eldin could do was watch in abject horror as the passionless butcher went about its business. He then suddenly snapped out of his daze, blocking out the terrible knowledge that each white body on the ground meant the sacrifice of a noble knight.

Unfortunately most of the other men and dwarves around Lord Arius seemed to be struck numb with fear. They were fighting at only a token of their true potential, as if the Sheul's presence sapped them of the will and strength. If not halted it seemed as if this one fighter was going to turn the tide of battle in the favor of the enemy.

The High King brandished his sword and rushed the evil creature. Almost as if it had known how Eldin would attack it, Lord Arius spun around and dropped to one knee, swinging its weapons as it went. Only the quick wits of the King allowed him to keep his legs as he jumped upwards, allowing his charge's momentum to carry him right into his enemy's helmeted head.

The shining white armor was covered in blood. Once the High King had landed in the dirt next to the stunned Sheul, it was further soiled with grit and dirt. Eldin sprang to his feet as Lord Arius rolled a few feet away and did the same. Now they faced each other, weapons poised. There was no need for speeches or taunts, each being knew that the other was an enemy to be annihilated. Lord Arius began to swing his two weapons in a figure eight pattern as he slowly advanced while the High King slung his shield from off his back and onto his arm.

The two fighters met in a clash of holy steel upon twisted metal. Arius rained a vicious flurry of blows upon the King, driving him backwards. Using his shield as a weapon Eldin batted aside the last blow, putting the Sheul off balance, and attempted a thrust at his enemy's side. Arius twisted his body away from the near fatal blow as he came around full circle with his sword aimed at Eldin's head.

The King just barely managed to duck the blow and from his crouched position delivered Arius a brutal uppercut with his blessed shield. The blow picked the Sheul up off its feet, lifting it into the air in a spray of blood. The heavily armored god landed several feet away in a jumbled heap.

A cry went up amongst the remaining knights as they rushed the fallen being, spurred on by what appeared to be a victory for their leader. The High King readied himself for the killing blow as he advanced with his sword gripped tightly. With all of his attention focused upon the prone form of Lord Arius as he approached, Eldin failed to notice the orc that was moving towards him.

Harrikan's blessings were upon the High King on that fated eve. Without realizing quite what he was doing Eldin raised his shield in a parrying position. Just as he did the largest orc he had ever seen took a step towards him and leveled its heavy blade upon his shield with tremendous forced. The shield held the blessings of Harrikan, but this was a darksteel blade driven by a creature whose one joy in life was the chaos of battle. The shield disintegrated as it gave way to the powerful blow, the force of which carried the blade deep into the arm of the King.

Blinded by pain and reeling from the shock of the blow High King Eldin collapsed to the ground. The blood-soaked orc, his savage face divided by a horizontal white stripe tattoo, moved forward and raised his blade again. Before the orc could bring the blade down upon the King he was attacked by two of the armored knights. The first knight made a clumsy slash at the orc's head, which the large orc ducked as he crouched under the blade. The knight's charge carried him past the crouching orc, but before he could slow his momentum, the orc came out of his crouch as he spun around, his blade cleaving the lower spine of the hapless knight. The second knight tried to skewer the orc with the point of his sword, but failed as the greenskinned warrior sidestepped the thrust and laid the knight open with a vicious upswing. The knight's body spewed blood as it fell to the ground.

The orc returned his attention to the King, only to find the white armored man blazing with power, advancing proudly with holy blade held aloft. The orc fearlessly attacked, aiming a powerful blow at the King's midsection. The High King easily parried the strike, letting the force of the blow carry the orc forward as he turned his blade over in a high arcing swipe that cleanly decapitated the brutal creature.

As the headless body crumpled to the ground Eldin turned back towards Lord Arius. Once his eyes took in the scene his breath caught in his throat as he witnessed the last of his knights cut down by the bloodstained sword of the Sheul. With a righteous fury the High King set upon the Sheul. Strike after strike he leveled against the evil warrior's defenses, driving Arius back before his barrage.

The sparkle of recognition glinted in the eyes of the Sheul, manifesting his knowledge about the immanence of his own death. Spurred on by his opponent's acceptance of defeat the High King pushed his assault. It was as this mutual knowledge passed between the combatants that a quick slash from Eldin's holy blade severed the Sheul's sword bearing hand. In the next instant the High King brought his blade over his head and downwards. The dark god brought his sword up for a parry, only to find that the entire hand was missing as the blessed blade bit deep into his chest. With a great shriek the ancient god collapsed to the ground, the sword cutting his blackened soul from the body even as the Sheul died. It's armor fell away in pieces as its body turned to ash.

With a groan of fatigue, Eldin fell to his knees only keeping himself upright with his sword as he plunged it into the ground and rested his head upon it. There he kneeled in relief and prayed as the battle continued around him. The dwarves and men found themselves at an advantage with the death of Lord Arius. The death of the Sheul prevented it from single handedly driving them off, and soon their superior numbers began to tell. The enemy fell one by one before the might of the alliance. The orcs did not retreat and were killed to a man.

The High King's head rose as he heard the victory cheers of his army. The dwarves raised their voices in song as the men added their much less resonant voices to the din. *Good*, thought Eldin, *now man and dwarf will be like brothers. United against the common foe in victory.*

Eldin rose to his feet as a group of warriors came towards him bearing a makeshift litter. The High King looked down in surprise as he saw what lay upon the device. It was an orc as tattooed and bedecked in foul jewelry as any orc he had ever heard of. It was still and contorted in the rigor of death. Several wounds could be seen on his body as well as two broken spears still piercing his flesh.

Immediately the High King realized that this must have been the mysterious orc wizard that had plagued and harrowed the forces of good for so long. It had often been said that Lord Arius would never have awoken without the power of this creature. Judging by its wounds and the fearful looks from the men who carried it, men must have died in droves to bring it down. The lives of good men and dwarves was the price of freedom and hope.

It was with this in mind that the High King raised his holy blade in salute to his army. The only gift he could give was his gratitude and devotion, a small thing for the guardians of good, though just enough to help them carry on.

And so it was that the alliance, lead by High King Eldin, the vicar of Harrikan, set out to rebuild the new world.

Chapter 17

Somewhere in the swirling chaos that was the home of the gods, a storm had begun…